NO REFUGE

BRANDON NOLTA

MONTAG

DEDICATION

For Mom –

Whose support made growing up a writer seem natural and right

Whose belief in my future as a writer never wavered

Who will never get to read this

CREDITS

"Aleph" originally published in *Stupefying Stories* (February 2014)

"House Call" originally published in *Other Days* from Jayhenge Publishing (November 2014)

"Toward Inevitable Dawn" originally published in *Quantum Muse* (May 2001); version that appears here was slightly re-edited and first appeared as a standalone story from Digital Fiction Publishing (February 2016).

"Fair Trade" © 2023 by Brandon Nolta

"Gray Eye Shuffle" originally published in *Mad Scientist Journal* (Summer 2018)

"Cloudbreaker Above" originally published in *Stupefying Stories* (September 2023)

"High Costs of Support" originally published in *Big Pulp* (June 2013)

"O Sing Me, My Muse" originally published in audio format in *The Centropic Oracle* (October 2020)

CONTENTS

CLOUDBREAKER ABOVE

Gusts whistled and tore at Chernin as she shifted position within the spiderwork of metal and expansion joints, trying to stay comfortable for a few minutes more. The last news she'd heard before leaving the ugliest building in the Erewhon said a storm was due around 8, and Chernin wanted to be hidden aboard the *Cloudbreaker* before the docking crew buttoned it up to fly across the ocean.

Steps from the rubber-coated platform overhead shook her perch, and Chernin froze. No docker would climb down among the support beams and shift absorbers to pull her into the coppers' cold embrace, but they could report her, have the blue and burly law waiting at every balcony and window in Empire Point. She'd have to come out eventually, but she only intended to go up. The trick was to avoid the crew.

Chernin breathed through her mouth, waiting for the dockers above to go inside. A cigarette butt spun over the top rail, and with a laugh, the voices headed away from the gangplank. On a calmer day, Chernin knew she could wait for the heavy thrum of the double doors closing, but with the rising wind in her ears, she could miss the sound and lose her chance.

The steps faded, and Chernin took a deep breath. Best to be quick, she knew, and began her climb to the platform. Too soon, she reached the platform's edge. Now that she was almost there, fear coiled inside her. What if she slipped? What if they caught her and threw her in a hole for daring to climb so close? What if she never saw the *Cloudbreaker* rise again?

"Idiot," she muttered, and cautiously lifted her head past the platform. Her heart sped up, and for a moment, the shadows from the docking lights and the iron sky looked like a knot of sailors, ready to grab her. She imagined how she would look to them: pale skin, shadow-black hair, eyes wide and childish, even though she was days past her 15th year. Old enough to sign onto Aerofleet, were she from one of the right families. Or any family. But the light shifted, and there was nobody there.

She scrambled onto the platform and crouched at the gang-plank's foot, scanning past its length for crew at the entryway, or shadows just inside. Her luck continued to hold. Clutching the canvas knapsack containing everything she owned, Chernin skittered up the gangplank into the *Cloudbreaker*'s starboard compartment.

She counted off the turns and passages she'd memorized from the plans in the City Archives until she reached the small nook, hidden behind piles of storage crates, that should be safe from inspection for a while.

Chernin sat back against the warm control bank and let out a long whispering sigh. She wouldn't be completely safe until the *Cloudbreaker* was underway, but getting on board was half the struggle. Dodging the crew would be tough once they left port, but Chernin had studied everything she could find about the *Cloudbreaker*. If anyone besides its builders knew this bauble of brass and chrome, she did. She could stay hidden, a mouse in the machinery, as long as needed.

Smiling at the image of herself with mouse ears and whiskers, running along the pipes and passages of the great ship, Chernin fell asleep, exhaustion and fear fading in the warmth and hum of the airship's pre-flight activity.

Chernin's first thought when she woke was that she was in a pocket of turbulence, a moment of shaking that arrived and passed before her mind caught up. Her eyes opened in the dim, off-shift light, the night watch standard according to every manual and wireless program she'd ever devoured. She listened for crew people moving about. All she heard was the hum of machinery and the click of switches.

Surely there was at least one insomniac on watch. Chernin stretched, yawning. Moving slowly, she stood and listened intently. Nobody walking by. No voices echoing down the hall, or sounds of bored card games, or whatever the crew did while waiting out the night. Chernin frowned. Years of stories had taught her that ships were never completely silent.

There was no help for it; she'd have to look. As quickly as she dared, she balanced herself on a crate and leaned out, her strong arms bracing her upper body. Her head barely cleared the crate's front edge, but it was enough. She glanced down the passage to her right, whipped her head left, and pulled back out of sight. No one in either direction.

A bolt of fear rushed through her. Had they even left? Maybe the storm had passed, and the *Cloudbreaker* was still moored to

Empire Point, waiting until they found the little Chernin in the walls. Chernin turned, ears straining, breathing as silently as her burning lungs could manage. Nobody behind her, no shadows edging near.

Nothing.

The cabin bumped. Chernin braced herself against the crate. Was this what flying felt like? She planted her feet wide and waited, trying to get a feel for the cabin's motion. Chernin felt the floor drop a touch, sensed the cabin swoop slightly starboard. She smiled. If the *Cloudbreaker* was still moored, it was a loose job. The vibrations and balance shifts said she was in flight.

One way to be sure. There was a porthole two compartments toward the bow from her hiding place. Actually, there were two, one on each side of the cabin. The porthole closest to her was by a crew station, but the portside one was in a hallway. That would be better, Chernin knew, but she'd have to cross the width of the cabin. *No point in daring the crew to find me,* she decided. As silently as she could, she crawled over the concealing crates and stepped into the lengthwise passage. She looked both ways and saw no one.

Five breathless steps later, she was in the crosswise connector, steeped in darkness. Chernin worked her way across, back to the wall, breathing in shaky inhales. At the portside passage, she darted her head around the corner. Nobody toward the stern, and with a sideways motion that hurt her head, she looked toward the bow. Nobody there, either.

She took a deep breath, strode across the passage, and put her face to clear cold glass encircled in riveted metal. Outside, inchoate darkness surrounded the *Cloudbreaker*. Chernin cupped her hands against her temples to block out the light. For a moment, the darkness refused to clear, until a cloud shifted to reveal a brilliant half-moon. The night sky resolved into a broken cloud layer above patches of glimmering water, and darkened land speckled with lights, over which the *Cloudbreaker* now sailed.

Chernin smiled, her reflected grin a dash of bright against the black. Her plan worked. An Erewhon orphan was in flight aboard Aerofleet's greatest ship, and nobody knew but her. For now, anyway, and her delight ebbed as she pulled away and scanned her surroundings, straining to catch any movement of the crew. She darted into the relative shadows of the connector, and willed herself not to run back to her hiding space.

Surely the crew isn't all asleep, Chernin thought. *Maybe they don't bustle around much, but there must be some movement. I need to know where they are, and how many. No time is better than now.*

The words, oft said by her nearly-forgotten father, didn't comfort her, but she knew their truth. In flight, the *Cloudbreaker* would never sleep more soundly than now. If Chernin wanted to explore, caution demanded she begin. She peeked out into the portside hallway, turned to face the stern, and crept quietly along its length, breath fast and loud in her ears with each step.

Chernin paused at every door and entry to check for shadows and whispers, and peered around each jamb and corner, searching for crew. By the time Chernin reached the galley, she was puzzled, but as she reached the engine room, with its rows of generators and turbines and capacitors, foreboding joined her confusion. Every room, every space aboard the *Cloudbreaker* was empty.

The urge to recheck the closest porthole seized her, but she forced herself to enter the engine room instead. Banks of machines, tubes, gears and devices, for which she had no name or purpose, surrounded her. A hum, low and soothing, buzzed against her skin, the heat of machinery and circuits. Chernin knew she was at great risk here—a platoon of dancing mechanics could be around the corner and she wouldn't know—but this was the *Cloudbreaker*'s heart. It should never be unoccupied.

But it was. After long minutes searching every passage and cubby, Chernin knew nobody was manning the engine room. The single most important place aboard, and—

Not true, she realized. There was one other place to look. Maybe the *Cloudbreaker* could fly with an empty heart, but not an empty brain. No ship could fly without a pilot, a captain. She had to go to the bridge.

Chernin took a deep breath, inhaling vapors of mineral oil and ozone, and turned for the bow. This time, she would walk the starboard corridor, hoping to find someone, anyone. Facts, measurements, irrelevant information surged through her as she passed darkened doorways to empty rooms, the moonlit night no longer as lovely. Each step echoed as she walked, past the crew quarters, the galley, a crew head, then another. Relays clicked, the *Cloudbreaker* hummed, but Chernin heard only her own noise.

After unending minutes, she reached the *Cloudbreaker*'s bridge, marked by an oaken door riveted with brass and copper, and an inset window rimmed in chrome. Chernin put her hand on the heavy lever and listened. The brass was cool, almost cold on her skin. She heard nothing.

Her father's words echoing in her thoughts, Chernin turned the handle and pushed. The door opened, revealing a fully functioning, clean bridge, decked out in the Aerofleet's finest decorations, and totally, unmistakably empty. Wherever she sailed aboard the *Cloudbreaker*, she was going there alone.

Dawn flooded the horizon, gold and pink against the empty blue sea below. Chernin had never seen such an explosion of color; by the time morning light reached the Erewhon, it was stained by soot and shadow. Terror had receded enough that she could marvel at the moment.

Her stomach growled, a hungry rumble in the silence. She'd retrieved her knapsack before falling asleep in the captain's great swiveling chair, and inventoried her food stores: two apples, half a loaf of bread, and a chunk of waxy cheese. Not the best breakfast, but enough.

While she chewed a hard yellow apple better suited for throwing, she considered her next steps. She had no idea where the *Cloudbreaker* was headed, or how long the flight. Her plans had been based around avoiding the crew, but while that problem was seemingly solved, she had different ones to consider. First off, how was the *Cloudbreaker* flying without a crew?

Climbing from the captain's chair, Chernin took a closer look at the stations arranged in a half-moon around her. Clean and chrome, they glistened in the brilliant morning as if the crew had just finished cleaning detail. Chernin had seen pictures and schematics, but never had the chance to examine the instruments personally. She approached slowly, careful not to touch. Her eyes scanned the controls, listing every function and measurement she'd come to know from the libraries and the City Archive, until she came to one she didn't know: AUTO-MATIC NAVIGATION SYSTEM. The light below the label was steady green in mute concert with the others. Chernin read the unfamiliar term again and again, puzzling over its meaning. She'd read of engineering systems described as automatic, but those were simple feedback loops, mechanisms that didn't require human oversight. Chernin froze in mid-thought. Automatic navigation: could that mean the *Cloudbreaker* itself was determining its course? She turned to the pilot's command station on her right.

And there it was, below the velocity gauge: AUTOMATIC PILOT SYSTEM. Bright green, like the other, and steady as the *Cloudbreaker* hummed. There was no trick. No mistake. She'd stowed away aboard an empty ship, almost certainly the first Aerofleet ship to fly itself uninhabited, maybe the only ship that could. No captain, no crew, one passenger.

All that effort, Chernin thought, *and I sneak aboard the only ship without crew.* Her laughter echoed around the immaculate bridge, bouncing off metal and wood. Outside, the morning grew in strength, warm over the ocean's watery expanse, and Chernin smiled as her laughing subsided. One constant from every conversation and complaint she'd ever eavesdropped on was that management was always ready to take shortcuts with crew wages, with a ready library of excuses to reduce bonuses or dock pay. A crewless boat would be Aerofleet's golden grail, then. No crew to pay, more room for freight because no crew quarters, and no—

Chernin's eyes went wide.

No galley.

Heart racing, Chernin bolted to her feet and ran for the door. Even as reason told her to remain calm, she rushed down the hallway to the galley, to the crew quarters, to the officers' lounge, any room that might hold supplies. After that, she gave up logic, and searched everywhere that might hold anything.

Noon came and went before a trembling, exhausted Chernin sat outside the engine room and accepted that other than what she brought, there was no food or water aboard the *Cloudbreaker* at all. The galley's shelves were bare, the freight storage areas empty. Even the plumbing had been drained. If Aerofleet was out to discourage stowaways, they'd found a sure method.

Chernin leaned back against the bulkhead as her breathing gradually slowed. If nothing else, she was safe from discovery. Little food and no water were the obvious problems. *Either I need to find both,* she thought, *or hold on until the Cloudbreaker docks. When is that?*

Captain's log. She'd found it earlier behind a stout but empty jug from England, but hadn't stopped to read. With forced calm, Chernin stood and walked toward the captain's cabin. Soon, she had the leather-bound journal in hand and was leafing through the pages, searching for information about the *Cloudbreaker*'s solo journey.

1902 14 May

Refit at Empire Point underway in preparation for maiden uncrewed flight. Tests with four-man Aerofleet scout Nike very successful, so Cloudbreaker chosen for first flight with complete automatic systems, despite my objections to setting sail with no onboard backup crew. High Command believes reliance on automatic systems with auxiliary Marconi wireless flight control will make for better press. Further objection on my part, it has been made clear, will meet with reprisal. So be it.

Nicholas Hardiman, Captain

1902 15 May

Dockside tests of automatic systems complete, with results green across the board. My own misgivings aside, Cloudbreaker continues to perform admirably as always. High Command has decreed the uncrewed shakedown cruise will be flown on an empty hull, so all normal amenities—food, water, crew accommodations, even the soap and flush tanks for the head—are to be emptied or removed. Once the draining is complete and the weather calms, Cloudbreaker will be launched, and my crew and I begin our mandatory leave. Six paid weeks off; the prospect of an automatic Aerofleet has High Command feeling generous.

Nicholas Hardiman, Captain

Chernin flipped through the remaining pages rapidly, hoping to stop the leaden dread coiling inside her, but Hardiman's entry on May 15th, five days prior, was the last. Six weeks in flight; with no food or water, she wouldn't make it to dock. She would die alone, a footnote in Aerofleet history, and the *Cloudbreaker* would be her tomb. Fear clawed up her throat and clenched her jaws tight.

I will not panic, she thought.

As she stood, the floor lurched a fraction to starboard. The light from the passageway dimmed to a shadowy hue. The floor lurched again. A gentle sound, sizzling in the quiet, rose from the passageway. Chernin blinked, and slowly, the realization stole through her: rain.

She turned to the cupboard where she'd found the captain's log, still open. The empty jug sat there, and Chernin smiled. *Too early to ready my funeral,* she thought, and grabbed the heavy glass container from the cupboard. An old smell of peat and hops wafted out when she removed the cork. Her nose wrinkled, but the jug was dry. She hurried back to the bridge, jug cradled in her arms.

After taking a too-small bite of hard cheese—*ration for now,* she thought, gazing longingly at the remainder—she walked along the forward windows until she found a manual latch on the port side. Gray clouds massed along the horizon, and Chernin smelled moisture on the wind as she opened the window. A sharp breeze blew past as she considered how to capture the rain. The ledge was too narrow to safely set the jug on, and holding it outside the cabin was dangerous. Plus, the jug's mouth was too narrow to let much water in quickly.

A patter of drops struck her, spattering her with cold. Brisk wetness soaked the sleeve of her shirt, and an answer presented itself. Rummaging through her bag, she found a clean, thin cotton shirt. She tied one sleeve to the window latch, hung the shirt outside, and closed the window as the gunmetal heavens opened and poured cold rain. Her shirt was soon soaked heavy, and she pulled it in and carefully squeezed water into the jug. With the window open and the jug uncorked, she retied the shirt to the latch and repeated the process again and again as rain pounded the *Cloudbreaker.*

Nearly fifty minutes passed before the last raindrop fell and Chernin recorked the jug. She hefted the water-slick bottle; about three-quarters full. Thirst sated from the rain, Chernin grinned at the evening sky and closed the window. *If only manna would fall,* she thought as she sat in the captain's chair, calculating how long she could make her meager supplies last.

Chernin found sleeping more difficult that night, even after nearly filling the captain's jug. Dreams of starvation and skeletons haunted her until just before dawn, when she startled awake in the slowly strengthening day. Chernin settled back in the chair, letting her heart slow to normal as she contemplated the days ahead. Fortune had favored her with rain, but she wouldn't have such luck with food.

Chernin stood up and began pacing, rubbing sleep from her eyes while she thought. Having searched the *Cloudbreaker* up and down, she knew there were no tools aboard, so taking over or disabling the automatic systems was out of the question. Manual controls were turned off; before falling asleep, she'd spun the tiller, flipped switches, and attempted to alter engine speed and revolutions to no avail. No tools meant she couldn't access or use the emergency valves, so shutting down the engines or releasing the hydrogen that kept the *Cloudbreaker* aloft was out. Chernin couldn't even access the wireless, as the microphone and tuner didn't work.

Chernin turned to look out the nearest starboard window. Far below sat a forested mountain range, sprinkled with snow and the occasional settlement. There were no maps onboard, nothing to indicate whether she was over Oregon or Oz. As she gazed over the wilderness, she saw a flock of white birds, arrowing through the sky below. *If only I could catch one,* she thought. *Catch, kill, and prepare one,* she amended, and shuddered at the thought.

For a moment, she considered what it might be like to cut short starvation by climbing through the window and letting herself fall. The gnawing in her belly was barely slowed by the small portion she restricted herself to daily, and when that ran out, the pains would only grow worse as her body ground to a stop, dying by inches. Starvation wasn't uncommon in the Erewhon, and it was always ugly.

Chernin sighed and forced the idea aside. *Chance and hope,* she thought. On the far horizon, the sun began its downward trek, and Chernin prepared her evening mouthful of food.

Chernin woke to a chilly blackness, only the stars and the internal dials lighting the bridge. She stretched, stood to get the blood flowing again. Below the *Cloudbreaker,* an ocean of darkness lay upon the world, broken only by the pale glimmering of snow, the liquid shine of water. *I could almost be sailing instead of flying,* she thought. *Surely the dark is as deep as the ocean.*

"A great flying boat," Chernin said aloud as she closed the window, and a memory shifted, a recollection of reading about the crashes and mishaps Aerofleet suffered in the early years, immediately after the War Between the States, before Reconstruction and powered airships made the South a rich tourist hub. Aerofleet lost entire crews to Caribbean weather and cold Atlantic storms, and installed numerous safety features aboard their airships in response. With the dawn of passenger airship travel, those features became standard, including lifeboats.

A burst of hope flowed through Chernin, warming her. If Aerofleet lifeboats were anything like the naval kind, there might be supplies. *If there's a lifeboat, if I can get to it, if there are supplies... so many ifs,* Chernin thought, but the chance was enough for now. There were bunks in the crew quarters, but somehow Chernin felt safest in the captain's chair, among the empty bridge stations and controls. Hopeful again, she let sleep steal over her.

Hunger woke Chernin just after dawn, the morning sun already vanished into gray overcast. A dreary day, but not rainy or windy; lucky there. Chernin doubted she'd be able to access any lifeboats from the main cabin, which left her less desirable options. Best bet would be astern, past the engine room and its works.

After a sip of water and the last bite of a heavily browned apple, Chernin squared her shoulders and walked toward the stern, heart pounding. Despite her excitement from the night before, every step felt like pushing through syrup, and her stomach—already afire with hunger—knotted into smaller and smaller compressions. She'd been all throughout the ship, short of climbing inside the envelope that kept them aloft. Could she have missed a lifeboat?

"I wasn't looking for one before," Chernin said aloud, and kept walking. She would know soon enough. She took a deep breath at the heavy engine room door. Between the eternal hum and buzz of the machines and the smell of lubricants and machined metal, Chernin knew she wouldn't be able to stay long without getting ill, so she hurried through the narrow spaces and rows quickly. Against the rear bulkhead of the cabin on the port side, she found a recessed hatch with the legend LIFEBOAT ACCESS stenciled in black. "I hope Aerofleet left them in place," Chernin whispered, and grasped the handle.

With a shuddering bang, the hatch flew open. A neat gray square of sky beamed through the opening, wafting in cold air. In the distance, a hawk soared among the clouds. A black rubber-coated walkway stretched toward the massive rudder hanging at the far end of the *Cloudbreaker*, a movable cross steering a metal cocoon. Thin rails ran the length of the walkway, and turned 90 degrees port to box in a bowed railing arching down from the top of the cabin.

Chernin grasped the edge of the hatchway and pulled herself partway through. A soft breeze ruffled her hair, and she inhaled deeply, driving the engine room from her lungs. She looked down, and a rush of dizziness flowed up her. Such altitude, and nothing but empty air below…

She closed her eyes tightly against rising panic. The world tilted, and she forced her breathing into a deep, regular pattern, ignoring the suffocation squeezing her. She opened her eyes slowly, letting her vision acclimate. The *Cloudbreaker* still soared, but her head was clear, and she focused on the walkway and solid construction around her.

Carefully, Chernin pulled herself completely through the hatchway and grasped the handrail on her left. She unfolded herself onto the walkway and stood upright, both hands firmly gripping a handrail. The wind swirled as she took one step forward, then another. Making the left turn at the bend took some doing, but she managed.

The lifeboat cradle sat at the cabin's midpoint, and Chernin was relieved to see that Aerofleet's scouring of the *Cloudbreaker* did not extend to lifeboats. There were two, stacked vertically, and covered with stout canvas skirts fitted tightly to pegs spaced evenly along the gunwales. Below the keel of the lowest lifeboat was a metal frame with hinges to keep the lifeboats from falling out. *Glad that's there,* Chernin thought, as she pondered how to climb into the lifeboat. Dropping the lifeboat down would make it easier to enter, but she didn't want to risk an accidental fall.

So, I'll climb, Chernin thought. The gunwale of the lowest lifeboat was almost even with the rail at her knees. By climbing over the handrail, she could almost step directly into the boat, once the canvas was unfastened. There was a gate that would simplify matters, but it had been locked for the shakedown cruise. She squatted and reached through the handrails; the canvas was firm, but the fasteners were made to be undone in a hurry. Chernin quickly uncovered most of the nearest side, and then it was time to do the part she feared.

Before her nerve failed, Chernin grabbed the arched railing and levered her leg over the handrail, straddling the top rail as she stretched out her left foot to catch the lifeboat's gunwale. The *Cloudbreaker* rocked gently, and she caught herself on the lifeboat. She leaned out into the clear air and found purchase on a seat in the lifeboat. With a soft grunt, she swung her right leg up and onto the railing, then stepped into the lifeboat and sat down, her grip sliding down the track without loosening. The lifeboat rocked lightly on its gimbals, and Chernin scooted toward the center, pushing against the canvas.

Once she got used to the slight rocking, and her heart beat at a slower pace, Chernin began to search the boat for supplies. They didn't take long to find. A compartment under the bow seat was clearly marked EMERGENCY SUPPLIES, and Chernin almost skinned her knees racing toward it. Trembling, she reached for the handle and gently opened the door. She pulled out expected items: flares, life jackets, a tightly stoppered metal canister of water, a waterproof journal with pencil for keeping navigation notes, and finally a series of steel cans with simple labels. Beef, peaches, potatoes. Joy bloomed inside her.

Putting the food aside, Chernin continued to empty the compartment. She began to inventory what she had, carefully noting everything in the journal. As the inventory lengthened, Chernin felt a frown grow. She reviewed her list, then every item again. By the third review, her frown had drawn into a grimace, her earlier excitement sunk into dread. For whatever reason—neglect, error, a prank—the supplies didn't include a can opener.

Chernin looked at the items arrayed around her, then at the blank sky beyond the *Cloudbreaker*. Tears pooled in her eyes, a laugh fighting its way up her throat. *It's funny,* she thought. *Surrounded by food I can't eat, stowed away on a ship with no crew. When they find me, I'll be a withered heap surrounded by plenty. Won't they laugh then?*

For a long, painful moment, panic clawed its way through her. She closed her eyes and tilted her head back, facing toward the Milky Way. A deep breath, then exhale. Again. Once more. Chernin opened her eyes. She twisted carefully in her seat and turned her gaze to the other lifeboat. White planking, reassuring in its solidity, hung above her. The metal framework around the arched railing was not as solid as she would like, but there were footholds and supports to grip. If she were well-fed, and not thousands of feet in the air, climbing would be simple.

Chernin reached out and grabbed a support branching off the starboard arched railing, moving before resolve or energy could fail. She pulled herself up the metalwork until she was suspended below the cabin's roof. As quickly as she dared, she released the fasteners along the side and peak of the gunwales and threw the canvas back. Chernin braced herself, and as she swung her leg over the gunwale, the *Cloudbreaker* bumped as if running over a broken cobblestone. Chernin gasped and hugged a horizontal beam as her foot dropped and slipped inside the lifeboat. She held her breath, waiting for another bump. The *Cloudbreaker* flew on smoothly, and Chernin slowly unclenched her aching muscles.

Keeping her right arm hooked around the beam, Chernin reached out and grasped the gunwale, wrapping her fingers around the thick recessed lip, then half-pulled, half-shoved her body into the boat, hoping that a last-moment swivel of the gimbals wouldn't cast her to the earth. Suspended for a long second, caught between the sky and gravity's embrace, she finally felt the scrape of strong wood along her side and knees, and even as the boat swung side to side, Chernin knew she'd succeeded. She turned around, crawling along the keel until she faced EMER-GENCY SUPPLIES once again. All she could hear was the thunder of waves, thrumming in her ears as air whistled in her lungs. With sure fingers and a jolt of wild hope in her heart, she opened the compartment door.

Nicholas Hardiman stood at the mooring dock atop Empire Point, watching the shape of his future change as the *Cloudbreaker* gently pulled alongside, settling into the locks as the Aerofleet crew tied the great airship to its berth. He raised his hand and signaled to the chief moorsman as he descended the spidery steps to the gangplank. Unlike many captains, he respected the dockside branch of Aerofleet and made a point not to interfere with their work, but a captain always had to board first. To Hardiman, that was immutable natural law.

The chief moorsman undid the hatch and lowered the steps, stepping aside smoothly as he did. Most dockside crews complied with captains' quirks, but Hardiman was liked and respected among the crews, and for him, their obedience was unforced and honest. Hardiman flashed a crisp salute as he approached, returning the chief moorsman's gesture precisely.

"Thanks, Chief," Hardiman said as he mounted the steps.

The chief nodded and started to reply, but Hardiman stopped abruptly on the top step. He leaned forward, sniffing the air. His hands tightened at the hatchway's sides, and the chief saw the captain's shoulders tense. Hardiman looked slowly around the inside of the cabin, peering at every inch.

"Chief," Hardiman said.

"Sir?" the chief replied.

"Step up here a moment, please," Hardiman said, and leaned to the side, one hand casually gripping the entryway. The chief bounded up the steps and met Hardiman's gaze at the top.

"Take a whiff," Hardiman said, gesturing at the *Cloudbreaker*'s interior.

The chief frowned, but the captain's meaning was clear, so he leaned forward and inhaled deeply. To his surprise, there was a smell, insubstantial but there. More surprisingly, it was a familiar odor. The chief had a full house of children, in-laws, and his wife, and it took only a moment to place it.

"Somebody hasn't bathed in a while," the chief said.

"Indeed not," Hardiman agreed. "But this flight was unmanned."

The chief gestured sharply at the ground crew, pointing at the cargo hold as the crew assembled. "Wasn't this a six-week flight, sir? There were no provisions on board, so ... "

Hardiman nodded. "The smell might have been worse recently. Let's search, but carefully."

They climbed down the steps and met the crew at the cargo hold entrance, outlining their suspicions and instructions in quick, terse statements. With practiced movements, the crew undogged the cargo hatch, swung it open, and boarded the *Cloudbreaker*, their minds on what they might find. A cursory search found nothing, as did the more detailed search Hardiman personally supervised. If the *Cloudbreaker* had flown with a stowaway of any kind, whoever it was made themselves scarce before Hardiman could discover them, leaving only the familiar olfactory evidence of effort and sweat without recourse to bathing.

Twilight found Hardiman standing alone on *Cloudbreaker's* bridge, gazing over the skyline beyond Empire Point, a maze of steel and glass and airship masts. Whoever the stowaway had been, there was no way to know; every trace had been cleared away. A diligent steward might see an incomplete cleaning, a hurried polish, but no information beyond that. Despite this, Hardiman remained unsettled. Someone had violated his ship. The fact that whoever it was had cleaned up after themselves was irrelevant.

Still, Hardiman admitted as the daylight turned to molten gold around him, there was nothing he could do currently. He would have to search again tomorrow, perhaps with the metropolitan police, who would surely have access to instruments of greater sensitivity. Thus decided, he strode out of the bridge to the cargo hold entrance, where he secured the *Cloudbreaker* against entry and turned for the captain's club. Thoughts of strong gin and hearty steaks occupied him, so he did not see the slim volume in his path until his foot struck it and sent it spinning across the loading deck. As he bent to pick it up, he recognized it as his captain's log.

"I'll be damned," Hardiman muttered as he lifted the book and flipped through its pages. His first thought was to wonder how it got here, but the answer was obvious. The real question was its placement here, and a few pages after his last entry, he discovered the answer. In a spiky, nearly feminine script, he discovered a message:

Your ship is a treasure, Captain. It was a joy and an honor to fly with her.

Hardiman read the two sentences again, then a third time. He looked around the loading deck and wondered where a stowaway could have been during the search. Then he looked down, pondering the latticework that stood between the deck plates and the streets far below, and thought of the skill and nerve it would take to leave this for him and risk discovery, much less climb under the deck and wait after six weeks alone, surviving on lifeboat rations and God knew what else, or find their way to an open window and escape inward and down to the streets. *Someone like that would make a fine addition to Aerofleet,* Hardiman thought. He smiled.

"Joy and honor, indeed," Hardiman said aloud, and left the *Cloudbreaker* at rest, docked in the night like a jewel tethered to the earth.

O SING ME, MY MUSE

After the crash, I explored.

Survival was no worry; supplies were many, just me in the courier ship, flying non-reproducible artifacts and *objets d'art* to wherever they go.

Boredom was my main concern. Communications down, and I'd forgotten to pack a book. Go ahead and laugh.

Then I found the jewel plains. Across bushes and sand, a shattered rainbow's worth of worn glass and metal. Time had done its work, nothing free of scoring by sand and wind, rain and sunlight, but the colors still beamed, erosion on every surface speaking something new. Against the scrub of an unremarkable desert world, everything looked made for the light.

Eventually, rescue came. A small jumpship pinged my rescue beacon, and swooped out of orbit within a day. The pilot bounded out of her ship, followed by a pair of medics and their silent med-drone shadows. They asked me some questions, confirmed my identity. All standard, but I was impatient.

When they finished, I pulled them to the edge of the jewel plains, where I'd set my studio, sheltered from the wind by the low rise that blocked the crash site. Out of pride, I showed them what I'd made: structures of light, rivers of molten color. Beauty, formed painstakingly in the desert light.

I turned to the pilot. Her face was ashen.

"How could you?" she asked, searching my face, my eyes.

"I don't understand," I said.

"Those ingots ... don't you know where you are?"

My confusion was answer enough.

When she looked at me again, I saw pity.

"Pieces of ships," she said. "Remains of armadas, and their crews."

"This moon," she said, "the final battleground of a horrific war, left abandoned as a warning."

She told me a story passed from politics, to history, to myth.

I looked at my hands, dusty, and strong, and profaned. I couldn't speak on the trip back to Iroquois Station. There was an investigation of exquisite politeness and understanding.

I was exonerated.

Reassigned.

This is what I know. My art springs from death.

They forbid me to return.

FROM SILENCE, SONG

None of the crew of the *Heaven's Path* predicted the hyperspace shear wave. Such an event had never been observed, and those few who understood hyperspace physics would have said it was entirely theoretical. Now, after losing nearly half the crew and a good chunk of the ship, Captain Drexler knew better.

"Options?" Drexler asked his chief engineer.

"We can enter the universe next to us, and that's it. Grav propulsion is gone, and the jump engines will soon follow. *Heaven's Path* is limping along as best she can, but we're in dire need of a dry dock. Best case, we'll be sucking vacuum in 36 hours," Lieutenant Commander Marrow said, the clench of her jaw her only sign of distress.

"That's the good news," Commander Chen, Drexler's XO, chimed in. "Bad news, we're parked on the existence boundary of a textbook Big Empty. Totally flat, hydrogen atoms equally distributed in all directions, no perceptible gravitational distortions. It's as close to a perfect vacuum as I've ever seen."

"I'll be sure to put that in the log," Drexler said, presenting his best attempt at grace under pressure. Marrow and Chen were fine officers, but imminent death tends to make even the best wilt, and Drexler hadn't missed Marrow's expression or the tremor in Chen's voice. "Can we evacuate the crew?"

"In a manner of speaking," Chen said, pulling up a set of diagrams on the conference room holographic display. "We have life pods, but no jump engines. The crew would just drift in interstitial space, and the odds of any ship picking up rescue beacons in hyperspace are terrible."

"Then there's the core," Marrow said, pointing to a power consumption graph with abrupt force. "The containment fields took a massive hit from the wave, so we're probably going to be without juice within 24 hours. That's if I can keep the failure from being catastrophic. Frankly, sir, not the way to bet."

Drexler sighed, and glanced at the communicator display on his left wrist, the dosimeter mode showing a number a couple digits too high. Drexler hadn't bothered figuring out how much time he had. It would be enough for whatever he could do, and then … it wouldn't matter anymore. He could live with that. So to speak.

"Are the life pods working?" Drexler asked.

Marrow nodded. "We have enough to support the remaining crew. All stasis beds report functional."

"An infinitesimal chance beats no chance," Drexler told his officers. "Life pods have some maneuvering and docking capability, so we can link them up, correct? Let's get everybody in a pod, eject them from the ship, band them together in a linked formation, and set one up as an emergency beacon screaming an SOS to hell and gone."

Chen nodded, though Drexler could see he wasn't thrilled about the prospect of going into stasis for what could be forever.

From the frown building on her face, Drexler could see Marrow had an objection. That was fine; it was the captain's prerogative to ignore such things.

"Let's get to it," Drexler said.

Chen and Marrow left the conference room, already giving orders to what remained of the crew. Drexler stayed in his seat. He was sure Marrow had caught his glance at his wrist. Even if she hadn't, she knew he'd been near the shear edge at Engineering when the wave hit. The likelihood of radiation exposure wouldn't have slipped her attention.

Drexler closed his eyes and pondered their options. In stasis, his crew had a chance, but the pods weren't smart enough to coordinate and link up by themselves, and there weren't enough experienced pilots among the survivors to make it work manually. To get all the pods linked and running together in real time, someone would have to stay behind. *Who better than me?* Drexler thought. *Captain should go down with the ship anyway; it's tradition.*

For a moment, he pictured how his death would come. He would run the jump engines for their final go, crossing the existence boundary from interstitial space into the emptiness of a universe doomed to stillbirth, a flat emptiness from a fatally flawless cosmic egg. Then, *Heaven's Path* would either explode into shattered debris, or peter off into death, his irradiated corpse at the helm, his last actions bent on keeping the life raft of his surviving crew from the potential high-energy sleet of *Heaven's Path*'s death.

"Computer," he said, "run a simulation with the following parameters."

Drexler fed the stats into the computer, followed by the conditions of the universe next door. For a few minutes, the computer crunched numbers, calculated variables, asked for clarifications. He responded, waiting for the machine to tell him what he hoped was true.

Finally, the simulation cycle concluded, and Drexler requested a summary report. The timelines differed, but for nearly all variations, the outcome was the same: the wreckage of Drexler and the *Heaven's Path* would disrupt the Big Empty equilibrium, introducing enough mass and velocity that eventually, an accretion disk would form. Given enough time, a star would emerge, and then, a stellar nursery could begin.

For the first time since the wave, Captain Drexler smiled. In death, he and his ship would ignite a new existence, the spark that began a universe. At that moment, already feeling the beginning symptoms of terminal radiation exposure, he couldn't imagine a better fate.

Drexler got to his feet and, whistling, left to return to his station and save his crew.

NIGHT'S OCEAN

Here, drink. It's fresher than what you spewed on the deck at any rate. The barrel moss keeps it clean, so I'm told.

That's right, take it slow. You were probably in the sea quite a while. We didn't spot any sign of your ship or your crew. What port are you out of?

No. I've never heard of that. Sounds Spanish. Are you a Spaniard? It's alright if you are. I don't much care about countries.

Calm down, mate, I wasn't laughing at you. This is an old ship, you're right. It was none too fresh when I first boarded her, and she ain't gotten any younger in all the years since. I don't know how many it's been, or the year of our Lord it is now. I've lost track of all the years, truth be known.

What's that you're saying?

No, I don't know what that is. I've never heard of a moo-vie. Tell me what that is.

I'll be damned. A magic lantern for hundreds? That must be something. I would like to see such a thing.

I swear to you, mate, I ain't laughing at you. I'll explain, but you won't find it funny. Just … well, what else can you do?

How long do you think you were in the water? Was it a few minutes, an hour? Was it a day? More? If you're like the others we've pulled out of the sea, I bet you don't really know. Go ahead, tell me.

That's what I thought. There's probably a good reason for that. Yes, I'll explain.

See, we've led something of a ... troubled life, you could say. We were a whaling crew to start with, based in New Bedford, and ... ah, it's in Massachusetts. Oh, you know it? Probably don't have a lot of whaling there anymore, but they used to.

Now you're laughing. No, I'm not joking with you.

Let me finish.

We were a whaling crew for many years, and we killed everything on or under the waves we could reach. At first, for pay, but over the years, more often than not, just because we could. Life at sea ... it has a way of making you see things in a colder light. That's the best I can explain it. If I were a more educated man, perhaps I could say it better, but there wasn't much schooling available to me before I went to sea, and there's not much in the way of books on the *Legend*.

Eventually, the whales became wilier, and our wallets got empty, so we went looking for different work. South to the Carolinas, on the trade routes to Africa. Ah. You've heard of that profession.

I don't appreciate being called a liar.

I don't know what year it is, I told you that.

Sweet Christ.

No, I believe you. Almost two centuries before the mast. That feels right.

Hah, I'm not a ghost, and neither are you. Neither are they, though they look it.

Listen, man. I'm trying to tell you.

It was our fifth trip to Africa, and we took a full load, more than full. We carried more of those poor bastards than any ship could reasonably bear, and before we were a week out, they took sick. The smell was ghastly, and their cries … the memory chills me. Then the wind stopped. We were a good week from anywhere, and for days, we floated on a plain of glass, nothing but the sun and the stars.

By the eighth day, half the load was dead, and the rest looked to be following close behind. No sense in waiting, or giving them enough chance to climb out of the hold. We chucked the lot of them into the deep on the dawn of the ninth day. Wind picked up an hour later.

Go ahead, look horrified. It was horrible. All we thought at the time was the loss we'd take on the trip. I know. I've had lots of time to think it over. I've had nothing but time.

What did they say when we got back to port? We never did. We're still on that voyage.

I know you don't believe me. That's alright. I wouldn't believe it. I didn't at first. We had the wind with us, and we made good time. The ninth day, we sailed like Aeolus himself was guiding us. Then the sun went down.

Maybe you haven't noticed because of the torches and the drowning you almost had. Look up.

It isn't cloudy; there's the full moon over there.

There just aren't any stars.

Now, lean over the rail a bit. Go ahead, I've got you.

Look at the water.

See there, off the port bow. Relax your eyes a bit. Look past the reflection of the torches.

Ah, you jumped; I know you saw it. No, I don't know what it is. Whatever it is, it's larger than any ship I've seen. It's not always there. I think there's more than one, but I don't know. None of us do.

Not much more to tell. Whatever took the stars took the land as well. We've sailed around this world more times than I have numbers to count, and we know where we are, or should be. We've got good maps and instruments, and before that damned trip, we could always find our way home. By your own numbers, we haven't seen land in almost 200 years, and may never again.

And neither will you.

For the love of God, man! Did you not see that thing? Don't even joke about jumping overboard.

We aren't alone in this damned night ocean.

It doesn't matter what you believe. Not anymore.

Might as well take a seat there. It's a long watch until dawn. Sleep if you can.

You're part of the crew now.

NEITHER RIVER NOR RAIN

The tide rises, and we may yet be free, if the world doesn't collapse upon us. I cannot be sure; my days beyond these rocks are long past, and I no longer understand mortal waters as I once did.

But you, my fellow captive, you I understand. Even as you gaze upon me from the deep, I know that you, who drink the sea thrice each day, must feel the changes to come. When you sing at night, long and low through the depths, your understanding rumbles my bones as the water warms and the jellyfish teem, even into the thinning fold imprisoning us.

I feel your thirst's deep bellow through the atoms of the water, up the bones of the earth, and into my ragged black talons upon the rocks. Across the choppy sea, the first signs of your long inhale appear. Since the folding, no ships pass through this strait, no screaming men to sate our hunger, so only I am privileged to watch.

The sea dimples, and the waves become scything arcs of foam. Water falls, spins into a pit, roaring foam and sea rending the air. I stretch my necks to their limit, waiting. Soon the maelstrom reaches its greatest depth, and…there. For a moment, your great baleful eye rolls, your gaze brushing me like sunlight. Every scale of my necks expands.

Too soon, the roaring fades as the whirlpool calms, curse sated. Water covers you again, and we are alone on different sides of the sea. Did the gods foresee this torment? I doubt the witch who poisoned my bath knew; jealousy alone was her motive. Yours, however...I feel he crafted vengeance from his lightning throne with an extra sting to the tail, as it were. He knew your heart.

Not that it matters. All the gods are vanished, and should the fold collapse before we are ready, we will be, too. For now, your thirst is quiet, and the worldfold shimmers out of reach. The seas of man are empty, although a large merchant ship weighs on the horizon.

I rehearse the spell, dredged over centuries from my curse-corroded memory, and wait. Tides roll and ebb, and the merchant ship approaches the fold, great metal boxes lashed to its deck. From the seafloor, I feel a tremble. I know the need is upon you.

Energy dances across my skin as the ship nears the outer fold. I begin the chant, ancient words strong in a dozen throats, my curse's deformity finally favoring me. The sailors and their machines perceive nothing, but the first parting of the way is a cool breeze on my scales.

There. If the sailors paid attention to the sea beyond their instruments, they would see the light change as their bow passes the folding. The spell is working, but I dare not stop. All my effort is needed to keep the breach open, as it takes all of yours to restrain the thirst. My voices shake, then steady. Ponderously, the bow moves toward you, and the spell gains strength.

I clatter my talons against the rocks, and roar.

Your thirst opens the sea. Foam deepens into the first arcs of the whirlpool, and a klaxon sounds across the water. Slowly, the ship tacks to port, away from your skirling curse. Toward me.

I trudge to the edge of the rocks. My prison has no shore, but we have spent centuries exploring every space afforded us, and I know how far I can go before the remnants of the ancient curse drive me back. Careful observation tells me the ship will approach just within reach of my longest necks.

Your vortex widens, and the klaxon continues to ring. Crouched down, I see painted railings inching toward me. Salt spray in my faces, I reach out.

The taste of rust in my jaws is sharp but welcome. I pull myself toward the ship, and another neck reaches out. A second set of jaws closes, and suddenly I am paddling, moving through a burning sea, brimming with salt and fading magic. Hoisting myself upward, I fall forward onto a plain of cold steel, and the last strands of my curse snap.

I lurch to my feet, a nightmare of tooth and talon and scale, and face a bridge rising vast and flat like a temple to the gods. There are crew on the deck, most frozen in fear or awe. A few use their weapons, buzzing like flies. On a balcony that rings the top of the bridge, a man stands before the windows, hands on the railing. His cap is white in the sunshine. Our eyes meet, and his thoughts are open.

Take me close to the maelstrom, I tell him, *and there I will leave. I will not harm you or yours if you do this.*

Calmly, he ponders. He handles the surprise well.

Your word? he finally replies.

You have it, if it means anything.

He nods at this, and shouts an order. They obey, and I coil myself at the point of the bow and lie down facing them, thinking of you. The maelstrom shrinks, but continues to churn.

Soon, I think, and hope our magic still connects us.

Quickly, the ship approaches the slow revolution of your draught. I know time is against us as surely as the tide, now that I have broken free. Of all our mad planning, this is the greatest unknown. Will we break free of this folded world, restored to what we were?

"My love," I roar into the wind. With all my strength, I bound overboard into the maelstrom's heart, falling as your great and baleful eye turns toward me, a tear forming in its corner as your gaze meets mine.

QUIET, THE TIGER LIES DREAMING

Quiet, the tiger lies dreaming in her bed, rails up to keep her from falling. The tiger's room is in shadow and soft colors, light blue and cool white, not her sigil hues of crimson, deep black, and violent violet.

The tiger opens her eyes, awakened by a streak of memory, or a sound she cannot identify. Though her mind is fogged, her vision remains sharp. Her gaze flicks to the doorway, expecting what all tigers expect in the rush and fury of blood. But that is not what she sees.

The shape at her door bows stiffly, at precisely the correct angle. Sinusoidal curves and artfully arranged LEDs shift in an approximation of humanity. The tiger is not surprised, not exactly. Even failing, the tiger still recognizes the gift to humanity that made her family's fortunes and elevated their names. Part of her, untouched by decay, believes her first design work may still thrive in this creature.

"Your medication," the shape at the door says. The tiger does not acknowledge the machine that glides into her room. Silent and respectful per its programming, it approaches the tiger's bedside. Even as her heart pounds, she cannot help noting the precise degree of deference the machine displays. The machine cannot be anything other than proper.

Spindly articulated fingers slip a pair of white pills into the tiger's palm. Another metallic hand, graceful but firm, offers a paper cup of water. The tiger swallows her medication, drinks from the cup, and sighs. She looks around her room, pondering. The machine waits, silently recording her vitals.

"Machine," the tiger says.

"Yes?"

"Do you know the story of the thousand cranes?"

A momentary silence. "Yes."

The tiger smiles. She is surprised by the warmth she feels. "Bring me paper."

The machine nods, backs out of the tiger's room. It does not find the tiger's request unusual. The tiger's days are most likely coming to their terminus, and keeping her comfortable until the end is its mission. It has noted many times that occupation with a hobby or activity can be of great benefit.

Pushed by focus and newfound patience, shapes form under the tiger's trembling efforts. Lopsided boxes, uneven stars, creatures with too many limbs or too few; the tiger creates, rages, throws them aside, demands more paper. Without complaint, the machine brings the tiger medicine, food, focus. It cleans up her destruction, studies her shaky but skilled movements, and follows her attention, patient and perfect in its solicitude.

Days vanish, visitorless, all driven away by death or fear of her relentless nature. Only the machine tends the tiger in her lair, writing her coda in data points, log events, and observations of medical value. Shadows lengthen with the season, and the tiger knows that time is short. Her life has narrowed to food, pills, sleep, and shadows, and when she remembers, she rages against the narrowing of her ending.

The tiger tosses in her bed, shoulders banging against the rails that hold her in. She wishes to get up, walk around, see the sky one more time, but her body is failing in sync with her mind. In her lucid moments, the tiger finds this funny, and laughs bitterly.

She opens her eyes, sees the machine sitting by her bed, waiting. The tiger has come to believe the machine gives her privacy, though she cannot prove it, or even ask most days. She reaches out. Gently, the machine takes her hand, as if lifting an eggshell. The burnished alloy is cool against the tiger's skin.

"For you," the machine says, and nods at the folding table clipped over her lap.

She looks at the tabletop, eyesight still sharp in the gloom. A glorious crimson tiger stands proud and ferocious, no larger than a matchbook. Precise, impeccable, geometric perfection that resolves into muscular shoulders, regal bearing, and a whip-lash tail. Impossibly, deliriously, she reads what she thought were imperfections along the predator's ribbed side, a second glance revealing them as the characters of her name.

The tiger turns to the machine. She struggles to speak, but the words are gone, even as the idea burns in her eyes.

The machine nods, bows to the tiger. It holds the tiger's hand, until long after the tiger has melted into the shadows and left her skin behind, long after the machine's work is done.

FAIR TRADE

I opened my eyes to a sterile lab. Everything was clear. Thank heavens this body had perfect eyesight; I wouldn't mind being without glasses.

"How are you feeling?" a voice to my left asked. I grunted affirmatively. Speech can be difficult in a new body at first, something about how the cortical implant handshakes with the language centers.

The table tilted to let me stand. I eased my way to the floor, making sure I didn't pitch forward. My perspective didn't seem changed, other than seeing 20/20, so I figured I was roughly the same height. I felt lighter, freer. Expensive way to lose weight. I looked at my hands. Caucasian male, apparently. Not my first choice, but for my purposes, not a bad one. I felt the back of my head, the bump of my special-request implant subtle under my fingertips.

Quickly and professionally, the implant people did their work: checked my status, got me somatically tuned, helped me dress, showed me the door. I reached the street, and found I was downtown. Normally, I would want to walk around a bit, let the sensory pathways finish aligning, but I was in a hurry. The GPS in my phone told me where I was going, and showed me the way. It even pointed out all 19 coffee shops I'd pass in the eight blocks of the journey. Marvelous.

Kev's people were good. I only made it two blocks before a nondescript gray sedan pulled to the curb, and two men got out as smoothly as if they were stepping off a bus. They weren't huge, but their movements were fluid and strong. I was sure they could catch me if I took off, but I wasn't interested in that. I stopped walking, arms loose at my sides.

"Come with us, please," the older of the two said.

"Do you know me?" I asked.

The younger man said my real name. He even got the accent right. Good for him.

"OK," I said, and waited for them to show me the next steps. They might want violence. I had no plans to offer any. Not to them.

The older man opened the rear driver's side door and motioned me inside. I sat down, trying to emulate their athletic grace, and managed to not stumble at the transition. The younger man sat in the back with me, while the older man got in the front. The driver, a younger woman in mirrored shades, didn't acknowledge my presence.

"Put this on," the man next to me said. He handed me a black cloth bag. I was surprised to feel the weight of metal. The hem of the bag held a glint of mesh and circuits, and my estimation of Kev went up a notch. A null bag wasn't common tech, despite the maturity of implants and switch mods.

"Please," the hired muscle next to me said. It was politely not a request.

I put it on, felt the circuit close, then nothing.

Reality returned in a snap, like someone flicked the world on. Everything was dark, with only the soft cloth of the bag against my skin to explain why. The cloth had a new bag smell, an absurdly cordial gesture.

"You did it," Kev said. I heard the groan of a body shifting in a folding chair. "Congratulations."

"All you," I said. It sounded muffled even to me. "I just showed up."

"Why did you?" Kev asked, and pulled the bag off my head.

A bright flare, then the world settled. I was attached to an office chair, hands and feet zip-tied in place. Kev sat in front of me, calmly watching me. He was in a matronly woman, a plump, blonde, older female who would fit perfectly in some Norman Rockwell kitchen, making cookies or sweeping up. The holstered pistol in the shoulder rig was, in the context of his body, an odd touch. Around us, four men stood at loose attention, casually scanning the room as they waited. Their weapons seemed much more appropriate.

"Chasing you is my only hobby," I said.

"I spent four years infiltrating your organization, and even I think you're a little obsessive," Kev said, his eyes dead in his grandmotherly face. "Is this about vengeance?"

I thought of my spouse, long since reduced to memory and grief. My brother in all but blood lost to betrayal. So many murdered colleagues. My life, my devotion to my country, cheapened, ruined by this…thing. I thought about everything I had planned to say if I ever caught up to him. Then I discarded those words. He wouldn't care, and I was ready to be done. "Yes," I said. "Completely and unequivocally."

"Refreshing," Kev said, and drew his handgun.

I laughed. Behind my eyes, I formed the first thought of a specific command sequence, then another.

"You're not bugged. There's no tracker. Your phone is en route to Des Moines. What did I miss, laughing boy?"

Carefully, even joyfully, I formed a third specific thought. The command chain complete, I felt a slow thrum begin to fizz through me.

"What did my implant tell you?"

Kev looked at me. I would know those eyes no matter what body he took.

"It's an older model. Bigger load, but viable."

"Ever notice how older tech tends to be larger, draw more power than the latest and greatest? New stuff tends to be more efficient, more subtle. Safer."

The thrum took a higher pitch. I could feel it in my bones.

"Implants are nothing more than electronic storage devices. Run a big enough current through one, well, there goes your data."

Kev's dead eyes went wide.

The whine in my bones became a howl. Kind of tickled.

"If you're lucky, this EMP will kill you. Not sure what an incomplete implant wipe would look like, but I damn sure wouldn't want to find out," I said, smiling.

Everyone turned to the door.

I laughed as the world ended.

HOUSE CALL

Tony rang the bell at the Dennis house, half-expecting a sheepish suburban man to answer the door and tell her they'd fixed the problem by finally doing what the phone tech told them to do. People complained about tech support, but most problems people had with their houses could be fixed with a handful of steps. *Like rebooting the damn thing*, Tony thought as she listened to the doorbell's clang.

A screeching howl blew the door open, and heat, dry and pulsing, baked Tony's skin through the doorway. Swirls of ghostly vapor blew around her, and a cold wind cut through Tony's uniform, dropping the temperature 15 degrees in seconds. Despite the annoyance, Tony was impressed. Even running on a fully loaded infrastructure, that kind of pinpoint climate control was tough to pull off without flicker or buffer problems.

"Somebody's been watching *Poltergeist*," Tony mumbled as she walked inside the house. Nobody was waiting for her; everybody was probably in the kitchen, trying to regain root access to the house, maybe bypass the OS altogether and do a factory restore. That could usually be done remotely, but once data capacity reached a certain threshold—and judging from the smartpaper and data ports at every wall stud, the Dennis family was way past that—problems like data cascades and rogue waveforms were best handled on-site.

"Hello?" Tony called.

Unearthly shrieks, and what sounded like an old Lou Reed album erupted from the room's corners. Tony's ears began to ring. After a minute or so, the noise cut out in mid-wail, and an exasperated voice shouted, "—in here!"

The whole family—both parents, two kids, a dog, and a grimacing older man, probably Grandpa—stood around the dining room wallscreen, pained expressions and looks of relief duking it out on every face. Tony thought of the combo as Expression #46. "My name's Tony. How can I help?"

"We tried to get the house into safe mode, but we keep bouncing back into this," Mrs. Dennis said, waving her hands at the room. Leprous red goop was dripping down the walls, and the stench of sun-dried roadkill overwhelmed Tony's nose. The dog, a good-sized golden Lab, whined and scratched at his nose with one paw. Tony crouched down by the nearest wall and poked at a bubbling puddle of red with her pen. It left a viscous coating, which Tony cautiously sniffed as a test. Whatever the stench was, it wasn't the goop.

"Cooling gel," Tony said. "How wired is your house? I don't usually see this much used gel outside of server farms."

"Everything but the foundation and the ducts," Mr. Dennis said. "I work from home, so I needed as much storage as I could get."

"The whole frame?" Tony asked.

Mr. Dennis nodded. Behind him, something skull-shaped bulged from the wall, like a head being forced against the wall from the inside. *Nice resolution*, Tony thought.

"Let's take a look at the operating system," Tony said, and turned to the wallscreen. She placed her hand against the lower-left corner of the screen and said the administrative password. Red goop continued to drip, but the admin menu appeared on screen. Tony clicked through several menu levels until she reached the process monitor, and expanded the window to fullscreen. At the root level, it wasn't hard to see the problem; several known malware processes were running, playing hell with the high-def drivers and the sensory outputs, and rummaging through stored files with abandon.

"Oh yeah, you're infected," Tony said, pointing out the rogue processes to Mr. and Mrs. Dennis, now hovering nervously at her shoulder. "Your firewall kept them from sending data out, but we'll have to clean these up."

"I thought we were fully protected with antivirus stuff," Mr. Dennis said, more toward his wife than Tony.

"Well," Tony said, "even the best AV program can't catch everything." While she was thinking about it, she pulled up the antivirus program from another level of the admin tools and checked the status. Yep, hadn't been updated in a while. Tony shook her head as she uploaded an updated definition set from her write-protected wrist drive. From the kitchen, a flood of rats burst forth, scurrying around her sneakers as she killed processes and ran the updated security suite. A trio of yelps echoed behind her as both kids and the dog retreated against the far wall, which was temporarily free of red slime and other manifestations.

"Your house isn't built on an old burial ground, is it?" Tony said, smiling.

"Thanks for recording all those horror movies last Halloween, honey," Mrs. Dennis said quietly. "Enjoying the hell out of the recap."

Tony bit her lip to keep from laughing. "Almost done here."

A handful of minutes passed before the security scan finished, signaling the rogue processes had been killed and wiped off the house storage. Tony double-checked the firewall and process monitor, and turned to Mr. and Mrs. Dennis. "OK if I reboot?"

Before either could answer, a shape made of tentacles and shadow drew itself from the floor behind them and loomed into the light, whispering in a slithery tongue as it reached for them. Mr. Dennis waved his arms as if he were scattering flies, his hands disappearing and reappearing as they passed through the holo-projection.

"Goddamn it," Mr. Dennis said.

"Yes, it's fine," Mrs. Dennis said.

Tony pressed the reboot command, and after several lines of text ran across the now-black viewscreen, everything disappeared, leaving Tony alone in an empty, featureless room. *Wow, even the dog?* Tony thought. *Those are supposed to be hard as hell to get right.*

"This is a really great setup," Tony said aloud as she wrote up the invoice for the day, wondering how rich you'd have to be to scan an entire family into storage, immortality in data. *Someday, maybe,* she thought, waiting for her customers to reboot back to life.

HIGH COSTS OF SUPPORT

The phone rang.

"Thank you for calling Invergent technical support. My name is Freddy; how may I help you today?"

Silence at the other end. The open line hummed, waiting for input.

"Hello, is someone there?"

No response. Freddy started a silent 30-second countdown, hoping he could end the call quickly.

"Hello, this is Invergent support, Freddy speaking. Is there anyone there?"

A crackle of electricity, followed by the crunch of glass. An indrawn breath.

"Did you say Freddy was your name?"

"Yes, sir. You've reached Invergent's support line; is there a technical issue I can assist you with today?"

Laughter, cold and soft, like a mallet wrapped in a sheet. "Well, Freddy, I've got an issue here all right. I don't think it's something you can help with, though."

"If it has to do with any Invergent product, I'd like to give it a try, sir."

"Aren't you a friendly sort, Freddy? I do have a broken computer here."

"How do you mean, sir? Broken in what way? We might be able to fix it over the phone if it's a software issue."

"Freddy, I don't know much about computers. That's a cold iron fact. I don't think they work too well with a bullet hole in them, though."

Silence. Freddy stared at the display screen on his digital phone. *One of the managers playing a trick on me?* It was an outside call, judging from the PBX designator code that came up.

"Sir, did you say bullet hole? There's a bullet hole in your computer?"

Across the cubicle from him, Jane turned around in her swivel chair, eyebrows high and mouth open behind the foam mike of her headset. Freddy looked at her, and Jane mouthed, *Bullet hole?* Fred shrugged.

"Yep. There is a bullet hole in this machine. Right in the side, probably about where the hard drive should be. It sparked a little after I shot it, and there was some smoke, so I unplugged it. It's not mine, so I'm not too worried, but I wonder if the warranty covers this kind of thing." The voice laughed again, and Freddy felt a chill.

"Uh, no sir, the warranty would not normally cover such a thing, unless there were special circumstances." *Jesus Christ, this guy's nuts,* he thought, and started scribbling notes on his legal pad. *I need a supervisor now.*

"Special circumstances? Well, I caught this guy trying to cheat me on a business deal. I came over here to discuss his betrayal. One thing led to another, Freddy from Invergent technical support, and I shot him. Two in the chest and one to the temple. To make sure. I would consider that special circumstances."

"Umm … sir, I don't know what to say to that." Freddy clipped the cord to his t-shirt, stood up, and began waving his arms for someone to come take this crazy off his hands. A sudden thought struck him, and he hit the Emergency button to start a digital recording that would run until disconnect.

"Ah. An honest man. I appreciate that in customer service."

Freddy turned to look around, and banged his shin on the file cabinet by his desk, knocking his coffee mug over. Instinctively, his hands flew to the mute switch. "Damn!" The switch clicked back, and the voice demanded, "What was that?"

"That was me, sir. I clicked the mute switch for a second to answer a question from a colleague."

"Well, don't do that again. I'll hang up if you do."

"I understand, sir. May I ask why you called this number? It doesn't seem like you need our assistance for a technical matter at this time." Staci, the day shift supervisor, walked around the corner of Freddy's cubicle and made a hand gesture at him. *What's up?*

Freddy handed her the legal pad and waited while she read his chicken scratch. Her eyebrows rose, and her mouth fell open as she read. She looked up before finishing, and pointing at his headset, whispered, "Are you shitting me? Is that him?"

The voice on the other end chuckled, short and chilling in Freddy's ear. "To be truthful, Freddy, I hit the wrong number on speed dial. I thought I was calling this fuck's partner in crime." Freddy heard a grunt from the caller, and what sounded like a heavy cloth bag falling on a wooden floor. "I guess he called you guys a lot."

"Sir, may I put you on hold for a moment?"

"Absolutely not, Freddy. I rather enjoy talking to you, much more so than, say, the law."

Staci was pantomiming now, her eyes wide. *Did you hit Emergency? What's the screen say?*

We're out of our depth, Freddy thought, making his own gestures as he spoke. "Sir, I certainly appreciate that, but you must realize this is way outside my job description. I don't know that I can help you."

"Don't sell yourself short, Freddy. You've been very professional so far, which goes a long way toward recommending your company for future purchases." The voice laughed again, this time a grating bray that rang in Freddy's ears, making him wince. "Besides, I can't tell you how good it feels to tell someone. I've never killed anyone before, though I've come close a few times."

Freddy could think of nothing to say. *I'm not trained for this,* he thought wildly. *Someone take this guy away from me.*

"Have I surprised you, Freddy? Horrified you? Frightened you, maybe?"

He said the first thing that came to mind. "Hell yes."

Another chuckle. Throaty, low.

"Good. I told you I like honesty. Not as professional as before, but definitely honest."

Freddy's tongue felt thick and dry in his mouth. He worked his throat, but couldn't call up any spit.

"Let me tell you, Freddy, it came as a surprise to me. I didn't intend to kill the fat bastard when I knocked on his door. Hurt him, oh yes. Beat him up, break a few small bones, but not kill him. He was too good at making money for that."

People were gathering around his cubicle now, some still hooked into their headsets. Every now and then, one would click off the mute switch, say a few words, and click back on. Sweat was starting to gather under Freddy's arms and on his neck, and he began pacing in his cubicle. "So, what happened?"

"Hmm? Oh, well as I said, one thing led to another. You sound like you need a drink, Freddy."

"Yes, I think I do." He picked up his coffee cup, drained the last few sips of cold coffee and cocoa mix.

"Better?"

"Yes, sir."

"Good, and you don't need to call me sir all the time. You can call me ... well hell, why don't you call me Fred? That seems to be a perfectly good name. You can be Freddy, and I'll be Fred."

Freddy swallowed once, trying to be as silent as possible. Staci was making her way through the crowd now, the site manager in tow, a short slim fellow who looked like he was working on a good case of heartburn.

"OK ... Fred. Please go on."

"Well, we argued for a bit, and it became clear to Al that I meant to beat the shit out of him. So, he pulled a gun, and threatened to shoot me if I didn't get the fuck out of town. He had balls, threatening me like that after a double-cross. I was pissed."

"I understand, sir ... I mean, Fred."

"Do you? Ever had someone point a gun at you, threaten you?" The voice seemed to drop in pitch, become a growl almost instantly. *Pit bulls do that*, Freddy thought. *Pit bulls and lunatics.*

"No, sir. I meant I could imagine what it was like."

"You say that," the voice snarled, but Freddy heard the anger leak out of his tone, like air from a balloon. "You can't know what it's like until it happens. It's unlike the movies, Freddy boy."

"How so?"

That chuckle again. "It was fun, Freddy. *Fun*. I haven't been that excited in a while. Maybe ever. I thought I might wet myself, waiting for what happened next."

Freddy closed his eyes. He didn't want to ask, didn't want to talk to this *thing* anymore, but it was obvious nobody else would, and while they were dithering around waiting for the cops, he was stuck with this madman who, if he was to be believed, had killed somebody, and all he could do was keep this guy talking. String him along.

"What did happen next?"

"He surprised me. He pulled the trigger."

"Really?" Maybe this son of a bitch was dying, too.

"Freddy, I'm hurt. You sound pleased at the thought." Freddy *heard* the bastard's smile. "It didn't matter. It was a .38 revolver, and the dumb fuck forgot to cock it. Goes to the trouble of buying it, and doesn't know how to use it."

A satisfied sigh. "But I do. Before he died, I showed him."

"I see."

"Do you?" Freddy heard the pit bull tone in his voice again, rising in his ear. "Do you really?"

Freddy sat back in his chair and pondered his options. Writing furiously on his legal pad, he motioned to the site manager and held up the pad, which said in big, scraggly letters: DID ANYONE CALL 911?!? The site manager nodded, Staci parroting him unconsciously behind his shoulder. *Great*, Freddy thought.

"Answer me, Freddy." Menacing now, violence in his voice. Like a .38 revolver in a small room might sound.

"No, Fred. I don't see, and I don't get it. I'm just being polite for the hell of it right now."

In the silence that followed, Freddy was sure the collective gasp of the listeners could be heard on the other end. *Hell, they probably heard that in the next fucking building*, Freddy thought. He started to write something on his legal pad, then threw the pad and pen down. *Fuck it. Nobody's helping me. I should hang up.*

But, he couldn't. He was hooked. He knew it, and Fred knew it, too.

Fred began to laugh, clear peals of sheer hilarity over the copper and into his headset. Freddy winced, and turned down the volume a notch, then another. *Man, this guy's just having a jolly time.*

"Freddy! Oh, this has been the best phone conversation I've had in years! You blindside me with the truth again," Fred told him, pure mirth in his voice. "Any doubts I had about today's event has been wiped away. I hope you're available if I ever kill anyone else."

"Don't make any appointments, Fred," Freddy said, and now he was the one snarling, all his fear and frustration rolled into his words. "You called a tech support number, not a psychiatric hotline. I'm not helping you now, and I won't be helping you in the future."

"Ah, but you don't know that, do you?" the voice asked. "You only know what I've told you. I could be anyone, anywhere."

"Me too," replied Freddy.

"Yes, but I could find you, generally speaking. Just as a rhetorical question, how many call centers does Invergent have?"

"Lots," Freddy said, striving to keep the lie out of his voice.

"Truly? Ah well, I'm sure that a large company like yours must have people all over the place," the voice said. Freddy knew that lie was easily caught; the company's Web site clearly advertised the fact that one call center did all the work, and that all support was done in-house. Making the best even better, or so the slogan went. Freddy wondered if this guy knew how to use the Web. *Probably*, he thought.

"Your point, Fred?"

"All you know about me is my voice, and I could disguise that, assuming that this is even," for a moment a clear Eastern European accent came through the copper, "my real voice." He paused for breath, and Freddy felt the beginnings of a shudder along his spinal cord, like ice at his neck. "On the other hand, I know who you work for, the department you work in, and your first name. I could find you, with a little patience and perseverance."

"You threatening me, Fred?" Toward the front of the building, Freddy heard a commotion of whispers and people moving briskly through the corridors. He craned his neck out of the cubicle entryway to see two uniformed cops walking his way, the site manager and Staci trailing behind them like a satellite of Planet Authority. "If you are, I will terminate this call, in accordance with Invergent general policy. Who will you talk to then, Fred?"

"Not a threat, Freddy. An option on possible futures."

"Not interested. If you want, you can give me your number and I'll arrange a call back for you."

The voice laughed. "Professional to the end. You're a man of rare talent, Freddy. We must talk again soon."

Click.

Staci spoke first as the police reached Freddy's cubicle. "Is he still on?"

Freddy shook his head. "Just hung up on me, thank God. What a sicko."

"You recorded it though, right?" the site manager asked in a gravelly voice. Freddy nodded, too tired to trust his speaking voice. Staci motioned toward a glass-walled enclosure at the far end of the building, where several runs of fat yellow cables could be seen disappearing into the ceiling.

"The switch operators will have the recording," she told the cops. One of the cops, a tall sandy-haired man a few years older than Freddy, turned and told him, "We'll want to talk to you about this call, see if you remember anything about it that'll help us. You going to be around for a while?"

"Yeah, my shift's over in half an hour. I don't think I'll be taking any more calls today, or tomorrow for that matter." He reached over and logged himself off the queue with a theatrical flourish. *I wash my hands of you.*

The cop nodded. "Yeah. We'll be right back."

Freddy shrugged. *Take your time,* his shoulders seemed to say. He took off his headset and flung it onto his desk, wishing he'd left early, called in sick, blown an eardrum, anything to not have taken that call.

"Jesus, what a sicko," he repeated out loud, looking around to see who might have heard. His cubicle mates had all gone home. Jane was the only one who stayed past three, and no force on Earth could make her stay one minute past quitting time. Until today, he hadn't understood that.

"I get it now," he said to himself. "Fucker threatening you shows a person the light."

He stood up to go talk to the cops, get the day's stress off his chest.

The phone rang.

LOADING THE SLING

I wasn't born a Belter, but I'm probably about to die one. Maybe someone will come looking for my carcass when the shooting stops, but it's not a good bet. There's a lot of us out here, and who cares about one more corpse in the dark?

For posterity's sake, my name is Ronan Daley, ore transpo specialist for the Osbourne-Chu Collective, employee number LX39942-A. Until today, I was part of a mining team stripping a hunk of iron and beryllium designated 32661 Hypatia. Everybody does everything on a mining crew, but my main job was slinging rock. Load the ore container into the mass driver, spin up the coils, plot a course, and let fly. Not that hard, long as you keep the data flowing so trajectories stay updated. Pretty routine.

Routine ended when the Blobs swooped in. They've got an official name recorded somewhere, something less offensive, but we call them Blobs. What they are is people engineered completely without a rigid skeleton. They can stretch and flex into extensions as thick as a trunk line or as small as a finger. A Blob envirosuit stretches with its occupant, and can manipulate surface charges to control machines, defend the wearer, or propel itself in a rolling motion. Watching a Blob race along a vertical surface is like watching water roll down a leaf.

I was down a hole when the fighting started, trying to excavate a stuck bit. Lucky me. Comms are supposed to stay open, but I swear a lot when I work, and most of my cohorts come from more prudish colonies, so they always tune my volume way low. I didn't hear the first warnings, if there were any.

By the time I came up into silence, the wave had come and gone, leaving me, and a passel of dead bodies on a dead rock. Blobs weren't interested in the rock or us; they just didn't want anybody at their backs as they pressed outward to the larger colonies on the Belt's edge.

My entire crew was perforated at close range, and left to desiccate in vacuum. The communications array was scrap, as were the jumpship engines. Given all the chatter I wasn't hearing, no point in shouting for help. I had air for a long while, food and water in the jumpship, and not much else.

But they left the mass driver alone.

After I got over the shock—I'd seen dead bodies before, but it still rattles to see someone you know cold and pale—I decided to do what I could with what I had. Revenge was my first thought, but I didn't know where the Blobs came from, and the mass driver's targeting system won't accept "no idea" as a destination.

Escape, though, was still an option. Rigging an ore jenny with a seat and extra tanks is an official Belter pastime. I figured I could probably get to Ceres alive. Within shouting distance would work. Of course, if the Blobs caught me tooling across the sky, I could expect a few shots on principle.

I thought about that for a moment.

Normal Belter funeral custom is to strip the bodies, wrap them in whatever's handy, and launch them to the Sun. Early days, it was strip 'em and ship 'em into the recycle tank, and sometimes still is; we're not sentimental about the dead. I needed my colleagues' suit comps more than they did, so I synced up everybody's suit comp and got them modeling all the trajectories I'd need, while I grabbed an empty jenny and set to turning it into a Belter Kon-Tiki.

After stripping the usable air tanks from my compadres, I retrieved the spares from the jumpship and jury-rigged some attitude jets in the jenny. A ping told me calculations were done, so I loaded them into the mass driver and started it up. While the loader filled jenny upon jenny with the last ore my team would mine, I maneuvered my ride into the caboose feeder position and climbed in, strapping up as securely as I had time.

I pulled up the HUD while the feed line ground and shuddered my ride up to the coils. Without knowing exactly where the Blobs were, I had no hope of hitting them, but I could make an educated guess. Not much work to pull up what asteroids were around, how close they were, and estimate the reaction a full jenny at top acceleration ramming a flying island might occasion.

"Hell, meet handbasket," I said, and keyed the launch. Acceleration pressed me back, then released as I reached cruising velocity. Even knowing where to look, my scanner couldn't pick up much at highest power. If there was an occasional flash of light among the darkened asteroids, it was almost certainly my imagination.

I'd have to settle for knowing the jennys would meet their targets, spraying ore and metal everywhere at ship-piercing speeds, altering orbits a nudge here, a spot there. Individually, not much, but in aggregate, navigation would be trickier for a while, and more dangerous. Behind it all, me and my jenny speeding along.

There's no happy ending to tell yet. As I record this, I'm still flying toward Ceres and a reception I can't predict. Maybe the Blobs have it, maybe not. Maybe I'll get shot out of the sky. Maybe one of these tanks is faulty. Even if all my calculations are correct and all the readouts are right, it'll be close, and I might have to get out and walk.

Whatever. I'll just have to figure something out.

GRAY EYE SHUFFLE

She looked like the kind of woman for whom doors opened. Tall, hair so black it absorbed the light, her body a pillar of muscle, she strode with confidence through the late-afternoon commuter crowd, used to being unimpeded. I watched her walk toward my car, and thought ghosting must have been a tough call for her.

She stopped in front of me, turned her head to meet my gaze. Her eyes were gray, so light they were almost pearl. That's just short of albino in the standard population, and rarer than hen's teeth, as mom used to say. In Lottos, though, that was almost base model. Eye scans are still the most common way to catch one.

"Double O?" she whispered, body tensed. She seemed poised to run, or maybe kick my head through the train window. I wouldn't blame her for either. Imagine surviving an apocalypse, or being descended from someone who did, only to find that you were now an asset of incalculable value, and everyone wanted a piece of you. Even the West was shitty about snagging Lottos, and they still had rights there. Allegedly.

"Yes, ma'am," I whispered back, nodding just a fraction. The whole point of ghosting was to avoid notice. Ghost suits work pretty well at deflecting attention, between the pheromone masks and pupil dilation sensors, but they don't do shit for loud voices or sudden movements. Keep calm and stay unnoticed.

She opened her mouth to say something else, and I held up a finger, pointing at the ceiling. Her eyes flicked upward to the sensor ring in the panel above me. She nodded, and inclined her head toward me, as if we were old friends, and not strangers on a trans-Bay of Bengal train.

"Next station," I said, yawning as I did. The older Sikh next to me didn't seem to notice the ghosting Lotto in front of me. He probably saw white women with smart lenses talking to themselves all the time. I stood as the train slowed coming into Chennai Port, and moved in front of her. No need to watch her leave; she'd follow. She'd need help to get somewhere she could be left alone.

The train stopped, and I headed for the door, eager to leave the train car I'd been in for the last couple of hours. Vacuum trains are about as fast as you can go without heading into space, but the Bay of Bengal is wide, and getting out of Myanmar safely is now more luck than skill. Bribery still works, but I didn't relax until we'd crossed into Indian Protectorate waters.

The station looked like every other one I've ever been in: cheesy holo-ads, clean enough to use without fear of disease, restrooms and snack bars every 100 meters or so. On the street, the pedestrian population was light, the bus and car traffic slightly less so. Chennai was in good shape compared to northern India, but losing more than a third of its population in two decades had left its mark. I looked around at the sidewalk, emptier and cleaner than in my childhood, and felt the ghost's presence at my back. I'd recognized her as Lieutenant Shrivani Chopra as soon as she looked at me, but decided to let her break that ice.

She didn't say anything until we reached the third and final alley in our walkabout through the city. I tapped a quick series of notes, letting the auto-lock read my personalized key, and stood aside, motioning her through the doorway. She stopped in front of me, looked me right in my ocular implant. "What are you getting out of this?"

"Money," I said. "What else is there?"

"Easier ways to get paid," she said, shifting her weight slightly. "Safer jobs, in places more welcoming to Americans."

"Am I that obvious?" I asked. I thought my mutt accent was better than that.

She nodded, eyes fixed on mine. If I hadn't known who she was, I'd have thought she was just nervous, instead of ready to beat my ass. Her resume made for interesting reading: the first front-line female Gurkha, so definitely armed, capable of killing most people, and—if a woman like her was running—in far deeper fathoms of shit than was healthy for me. Which brought me back to her question.

Carefully, I reached up and pulled the smart lenses off my face. Just for show, anyway.

"This one's fake," I said, tapping my left eye with my finger. The iris folded outward, revealing circuitry, which didn't seem to surprise her. "This one's not." I pulled back my eyelid, and quickly hooked the colored contact lens out. Simple but effective, even though any scanner will look past the lens. If they don't think to look, it doesn't matter how good the scan is.

I blinked a couple of times, and met her gaze, the Lotto gray of my real eye matching hers.

Lieutenant Chopra blinked once, twice. Then she smiled.

"Shall we?" I asked.

Together, we went inside to begin sneaking an immortal lieutenant out of India.

When the genetic anomalies first started to show up, lots of people thought the stories were bullshit, cooked up by governments too afraid to admit how bad things really were. Losing nearly two billion people will do that. It didn't take long for rumor to become documented fact, though.

After years of battle with gene-bombs, crude nanotech, and whatever the skunk works of various nations came up with, the world was left with mountains of corpses and, like a rare orchid growing in a landfill, a new strain of humans. Lottos, they were called, because they'd struck the genetic jackpot: an immune system that could stave off death. Supercharged lymphatics, cells that breezed past the Hayflick limit without metastasizing, every filter and recycling system in the body cranked up to just short of magic. Lottos could eat trash without problems and drink a mug of Ebola and maybe get a temporary rash, while a needle full of HIV did nothing at all.

Of course, they were still vulnerable to the usual. Fire, bullets, plane crashes, and knives would kill a Lotto just as dead as a regular human. Or so everyone thought, until a Lotto in Johannesburg walked out of a hospital morgue four hours after dying in a hotel fire, naked and surprised but apparently unharmed. Short of completely dismembering the brain, a Lotto could heal from damn near anything. After that discovery, Lottos became hunted, and I found a new career.

A person grows up military like I did, and they get used to making their way around quick. I discovered that if you have a talent for languages, a face made for ghosting, and the ability to speak softly until you need the big stick, smuggling might be for you. There's money in moving everything from cigarettes to prosthetics, but the serious money is in moving Lottos to one of the three safe places left: Australia, New Liberia, or Taiwan. My client, once a cultural attaché based in Sydney, knew where she wanted to go, and for the money she paid, I was going to get her there.

We walked inside the tin-walled hideaway and entered a long hallway connecting to a dozen other shacks, huts, and occasional real buildings. I led her through the maze, navigating by smell and memory, until we found Aziq's shop. It looked like any other door, although a little more purple than the rest, but my artificial eye picked up the flycams and tripwires easily enough. Probably meant there were traps I couldn't see. I made sure to approach slowly, with cash and ID easily visible in the mottled sunlight entering through gaps in the roof.

I heard a clicking sound, and from the way she shifted, so did my client. "Double O, who's your friend?" a voice asked.

"Fellow traveler," I said. "Needs some vacation time."

"We aim to please," the voice said, and Aziq's purple door swung open. Together, my client and I strode in, letting our eyes adjust to the lack of illumination in Aziq's shop. Shelves of random parts, LEDs, and devices too damaged to identify were propped against the walls, reaching to the ceiling, maybe holding it up. Every flat surface was piled with technical manuals, newsprint, food wrappers, and well-used tools, and one wall was almost completely covered with scavenged plasma and LCD monitor screens. The floor was wall-to-wall static matting, spotlessly clean and almost glistening.

"Just for show," my client said, looking at the floor. I nodded. She had a good eye. Aziq's real business was a little deeper into the rat's nest.

"Aziq's in the blending business," I said.

My client reached to her left and knocked a stack of old wrappers and what looked like Soviet-era invoices onto the floor, sending up a pillar of pale dust. The mess scattered over the floor, carpeting the entryway in old paperwork.

"Glad to help," she said.

I smiled, and led her back to Aziq's real shop. Behind a ratty tapestry that Gandhi might have had in his youth, a hermetically sealed door was jammed into the wall. The sensor plate scanned us, and we were rewarded with a whoosh of pressure as the door opened. Holding the door open for my client, I followed her inside.

"Lieutenant Chopra, it's an honor to meet you," Aziq said, bowing slightly as he spoke. His bald head seemed to glow in the fluorescent light. Around us, a ring of 3-D printers and blade racks loomed from ceiling to false floor, under which snaked miles of cables and connections. Rumor was, Aziq had the fifth-largest data center in eastern India.

"You know who I am?" my client asked. Her expression was pleasant, but her eyes were hard. I remembered that I didn't know where her kukri was, or if she had more than one of those curved blades at hand.

"I worked with a company of Gurkhas in Sri Lanka, some time ago. Your op in Pakistan was popular water cooler gossip for a time. You have more friends than you know, lieutenant."

She smiled. "Maybe I'll meet them someday."

Aziq smiled in return, the corners of his mouth barely twitching under his meticulously groomed mustache. "All good things in due time. Come, please have a seat. The databank search may take a few more minutes. You may as well be comfortable."

Lieutenant Chopra and I sat in battered office chairs for the better part of two hours, watching Aziq in his element, hiding searches and back-door data dumps behind a forest of shell accounts, zombie accesses, and the occasional social engineering hack. I barely recognized half of the techniques and tricks he used, but I knew enough to realize I was watching a forger's Michelangelo, whittling a new life from a block of data and bureaucracy. Whatever the lieutenant thought, she kept to herself. Slowly, my client's new identity, clean and free of any reason for government attention, took shape in Aziq's hands.

As evening fell, the last forgery emerged from the printer, and we were done. Physically, we weren't buying much: a few smart docs, a passport with ID chip, and a couple of bankcards hooked to artificially aged accounts. Aziq bowed as I paid him, and walked us out through a different door. When we stepped outside again, we were three blocks north of the alleyway.

"How far can we trust these?" she asked me as we walked toward a bus kiosk. Street buses still took cash, and I figured we had to wait an hour or so to let the new ID wend its way through Protectorate systems.

"Aziq hasn't screwed a client yet, but let's not push it. Your face is still relatively well-known, and a ghost suit won't do diddly against high-focus surveillance."

"No shopping sprees, then."

"No," I laughed.

She looked down the road at the wheezing metal box making its way toward us. Looked like it still used diesel, and might have been brought by the British. Still, it was mostly empty, and wouldn't have much surveillance. "How do you plan to get us out of the country?"

"Hope you don't get seasick."

Lieutenant Chopra didn't look thrilled. I made a note to give her Dramamine before she boarded the cargo ship. She didn't know how fortunate she was, getting to ride in a tub with actual passenger compartments, but telling her that probably wouldn't help.

With a clank and a whoosh of exhaust, the rickety bus stopped, and the driver, who was old when the bus was new, cranked open the door. We climbed aboard, and found seats toward the back, a couple rows behind a quiet family, and a sullen city policeman uninterested in anything but sleeping.

I went over the plan again as the bus lurched back onto the road. Arrangements to ship the lieutenant out on a New Liberia-registered cargo ship were set, but the captain would need an additional bribe to not turn my client in. Once the ship entered international waters, I'd trip an Aziq special: an alert that the lieutenant was seen in a little cafe near Jammu, close to Pakistan. Maybe the Protectorate goons would buy it, but either way, it would muddy the waters. Once the ship reached Jakarta, a fisherman friend related to half of Java would pick her up and island-hop her all the way to Papua New Guinea, then put her on a private flight into Sydney. I'd had clients successfully make this trip before, so I was only mostly worried.

"Two questions," she said as the bus turned onto the wide road to the docks. I nodded; most clients were not as cooperative, so I felt like I owed her a little something.

"What does Double O stand for?" she said.

"Othello," I said. "My dad heard the name once, thought it was great for a girl."

"Did no one point out the character is a man?"

"He didn't care about that. Finding out the original was Black, something else."

She laughed, a low throaty sound that didn't carry far. The policeman stirred in his seat, then slumped against the window again. I looked at the road ahead. In the distance, I could see the stop approaching, and beyond that, the entrance to the cargo docks, where some of our fellow riders were likely going to work.

"Very well, Othello. Your given name is far better than your nickname."

"There's another meaning to it. It comes from an old movie series, something about spies. My parents thought it was funny."

She nodded, pursed her lips. I thought I knew what her second question might be. Proving my Lotto nature was usually good enough, but I suspected my proof would raise another issue.

Before she could frame the question, the bus chuffed and rattled to a stop at the first dockside station. We got to our feet and shuffled down the aisle. Nobody looked twice. The policeman slept through the entire stop.

I started to walk toward the docks, mentally counting off the ships until we reached the New Liberian freighter, and a firm hand closed around my upper arm. My client looked sternly at me. My krav maga is good, but not good enough. I waited.

The lieutenant took a deep breath. "Why are you lying about being a Lotto?"

I thought about how to answer. Damn, she was observant. Wrong conclusion, but she didn't have all the info. I put my hand over hers. "I didn't lie, Lieutenant. You just don't have the whole picture."

"Explain, please," she said, in a tone that didn't sound like a request.

Gently, I took her arm. "I'll do better. Come on."

I led her around the side of the squat office building that fronted the main entrance. We walked to the first door, which opened to reveal a dilapidated restroom. An "out of order" sign was nailed to the door, but that was fine. I'd scouted this place; it had lights and a mirror, which was all I needed. I ushered her inside and locked the door behind us.

"I'm going to reach inside my pack now," I said. "I assume you have a kukri on you?"

"Two," she said.

"OK, well, you don't need them. Just watch," I said.

I took out my med kit, unrolled it on the counter next to the sink. By habit, I inventoried what I had: three full vials of my latest compound, a hypogun, a full set of surgical scalpels, and two packs of disinfectant. More than enough, as long as I got the mix right. Too little methotrexate, too much generic glucocorticoid, things could get uncomfortable.

"Let's not assume anything here. Why do you think I'm not a Lotto?" I asked as I loaded a vial into the hypogun.

"Your artificial eye," she said, gaze locked onto my arms and shoulders. Waiting for me to grab for something, I figured.

"Because it would regrow, right?" I said. "Even if I'd lost the eye before those genes went active." I swabbed a patch on my upper arm, and pressed the hypogun nozzle against my skin. The trigger fired automatically at the correct pressure, made to be as idiot-proof as possible. Lieutenant Chopra nodded.

"Therefore," I said, "if I have an artificial eye, I'm not a Lotto, no matter what other signs may present. My eye color could be due to albinism or injury, and some conditions can mimic common Lotto genetic expressions. Logical?"

"I agree," the lieutenant said.

"Best disguise there is for a Lotto," I said, washing my hands in disinfectant. The scalpels got a heavy spray, and a quick scan confirmed the blades were as clean as could be in a Chennai restroom without plumbing. My real eye couldn't do that.

"Lotto traits often run in families," I said. "Any of your family come up lucky besides you?"

"No, though I had an uncle who disappeared suddenly when I was in training," she said thoughtfully. "I am the first confirmed."

"My parents didn't have it," I said, holding a scalpel up to the light. "My brother did, though." I handed her the scalpel handle first to hold while I went through the removal procedure for my artificial eye. "So did my daughter."

She breathed in sharply, but said nothing. Nothing to say, really. Many normal people had similar tales; Lottos just had them with a side order of dread. Every time I looked at other

Lottos, I couldn't help but see her face, her eyes, hear her infant cries as they pulled her from my arms.

"Hold this so that it faces me," I told her. "This mirror is filthy."

Lieutenant Chopra did as I said. The wireless connection was good; I could see myself clearly, including the ocular tissue regrowing along the interior wall of the socket. From the tingling in my fingers, the immunosuppressants were taking effect. I still had another minute or so before I could switch out the vials and shoot analgesic spray into the socket. One of the downsides of being a Lotto is that painkillers don't work well. For what was next, though, painkillers were essential. My knowledge was hard-earned.

The tingling turned into a low hum, not unpleasant, but strange. I loaded the analgesic into the hypogun, turned the setting to spray, and coated the interior of my eye socket. Then I did it again. Cold needling turned to numbness, and within a few seconds, it was as if the socket was no longer there.

"Between the immunosuppressants and my artificial eye's housekeeping, I can keep the eye from coming back quickly," I told her as I pulled a pair of micro-forceps from the med kit. "I am a Lotto, though. It will grow back, and the cocktails only work for so long. Mixing a new compound takes time."

"And so..." the lieutenant began.

"And so," I said, "occasionally, I have to cut."

Gently, I reclaimed the scalpel from my unwitting assistant. I pressed the blade against the socket rim, checking for sensitivity to pressure or cold. Good to go.

"We'd better hurry," I said. "Your ship leaves soon."

TOWARD INEVITABLE DAWN

Davis Manning stared through his reflection in the airport window, not seeing the desert-edge sunshine outside, and thought about the world that used to be. An errant breeze ruffled the tangled locks peeking out from underneath his near-shapeless cap. Overhead, the twisted beams that once held a metal ceiling cast shadows against the floor.

His companion rose from the plastic seat next to him and stood at his shoulder. Born just before the Change, she always seemed to him to carry an oddness about her, like a static charge. Three years ago, her family had asked him to train her, and they'd traveled together ever since. This didn't strike him odd at the time, but thinking about it later, he wondered at their motives. It didn't make much difference now.

"Are they near?" the girl asked. She scanned the low mountains at the edge of the burn zone, wary but not afraid. She'd learned well, faster than him in many respects. Since her family was gone, slaughtered in a fire raid shortly after they met, he felt proud of her in their stead.

"Doubtful. They tend to stay away from these ruins, let time do their work for them. They're a patient race." He focused on the sky again, looking for wings. "They respect this place more than the city around it. Still, we can't stay here forever."

"They have our smell in their hearts." The statement was flat, her voice hard. He nodded, knowing without looking her eyes would be the same.

"Let's move on to the tubes. We'll talk about our next foray after we've rested and resupplied." The man did not wait to see if she would agree before turning and striding down the ruined length of the concourse, his nearly depleted pack slung across his broad shoulders. She was a skilled hunter, and he knew she would strike out on her own soon.

Her footsteps fell into place beside him, and he smiled. Perhaps he wasn't ready to be alone again just yet.

Inside the main terminal, the insulating shadows hid the heat. Outside, the desert heat surprised him with its bite. Waves shimmered the air, rippling the time-battered tarmac where turbines once pushed men into the air. He remembered flying on a jetliner in his college days. It had been a terrifying experience, and would probably always be his one brush with flight. He saw the burnt wreckage of a passenger plane at the edge of a runway, summer flowers and weeds sprouting around the blackened struts and slivers of metal, and remembered.

"I would like to fly, someday," the girl said as they passed the wreck. Her voice sounded wistful, a reminder that she was still barely an adult by Davis' standards. "We still have the remembering of it, don't we? It hasn't been that long for us."

"Yes," he agreed, as they crossed the black asphalt ribbon and reached the dust plain at the airport's edge. Pulling the cap tighter over his head, he shaded his eyes and looked out past what was once a National Guard base, scanning for a marker. *There it is. Thank God, wherever He went.* "The technology still exists, and the remembering of it. We haven't lost that at least, just the ability to use it. We'll get it back someday. Maybe we'll both see it happen."

She smiled at that. He smiled back; he'd forgotten how pretty she was. He shook his head, laughing at himself. Before the Change, things like that could get you in trouble. Not many people cared anymore. In his darker moods, he thought that might be worse than the Change itself.

They headed into the desert together, away from the ruins of the airport and the city it once serviced. Behind them, the airport sat mute, surrounded by broken glass and carbonized metal, a corona of silence. On one relatively unbroken wall, there was a spray-painted message, faded but still legible under the grime and ash streaks. The man thought it a good epitaph, but the girl simply laughed, a short bitter bark, and continued past.

It read: *Here there be dragons.*

*   *   *

At the check-in gate, a massive hodgepodge of sheet metal and cinderblock slabs strung together with steel cabling, the hunters were met by a short, brown-haired man who hardly looked old enough to shave. Had the guard not been carrying a battered but well-maintained M-16, Davis might have laughed. The girl was simply bored. She'd grown up in a similar armed commune, and was used to guns.

"Your business, stranger?" the guard asked, voice steady, and dark eyes fixed on Davis alone. That was no surprise. This was

Mormon country, and had been since before the Change. Good thing, too. More than once, guards ignoring his companion had come in handy.

"Rest and resupply. We've been wandering the desert between here and the Wasatch Range for several months, and could use some extra stock."

The guard's eyes flicked to the girl, then flicked back. Davis suppressed a sigh. Usually, someone would say something, or make an unwanted move, and that was when the trouble would start. He hoped to be out of there before anyone had a chance. Manning took a deep breath, enjoying the subterranean chill. Like many camps in the area, this one was carved out of an ancient lava tube, cold thousands of years before man arrived.

Suddenly, the man smiled, and stood aside. "Then come in, and welcome to New Provo." He bowed, and waved at the door-keeper to unbar the gate. With a thrumming of cable tension and a few showers of crumbled cement, the gate swung open, and the hunters walked inside. The actinic glare of a sodium-vapor streetlamp shone down from the top of a pillar, throwing their shadows into sharp relief against the igneous walls. Another guard, an older man with a livid burn scar across his forehead, stood at the end of the entryway with a clipboard in hand. Both hunters unholstered their firearms slowly to check them in.

The guard cocked an eyebrow as the older hunter placed his pistol, a chrome-finished .44 Magnum, next to his .280 hunting rifle in a salvaged gun rack, US ARMY barely visible on one olive-green side. When the girl placed her weapons in the cabinet, a 30/.06 and a .357 revolver, the eyebrow went higher still. He looked at them closely, a question in his eyes. Manning nodded, and offered his arm to the guard. Feeling the sleeve of the hunter's longcoat, he whistled once, long and low in disbelief. "That really what I think it is?"

Manning nodded. "Took it down about a year ago in a river canyon. Waited at the canyon lip until it made a pass for water, then caught it in crossfire. They look heavy, but they float pretty well."

"You sound experienced." The guard's eyes were wide with respect. Scavengers and wanderers were common, but successful dragonhunters were few and far between.

"Too much experience, I'm afraid. I'll gladly forget it all when they're gone." Davis signed his name on the clipboard. "Do you have ammo for trade here?"

"Go to the gunsmith, about two hundred yards down the main tube and to the left. He and his family managed to salvage nearly everything usable from the National Guard base after the first attacks. If there's any ammo of that kind to be found here, the Allyn clan will have it, Mr. —" the guard glanced at his clipboard, "—Manning." He handed the hunters their weapon tags. "Ask anyone if you need assistance. We're pretty friendly here in New Provo."

"Thanks," Manning said. He slid the tags into an inside pocket, carefully avoiding the serrated edges of the clasp made from the canines of the same beast he was wearing. Pickpockets were common, even in orderly Mormon communes. Sometimes Manning thought the Change only deserved a lower-case c.

"Here are your tags, Miss. Enjoy your stay in New Provo."

The girl, who'd only signed in as Raven, said nothing. She took her tags and headed for the gunsmith, eager to transact their business, get a night of rest and leave. Manning followed a step or two behind, wondering who would start the fight this time, and if he could get enough supplies before they did to make it to the Oregon border.

New Provo's marketplace was much like the countless others Manning had wandered over the years: crowded and busy, but quiet, as if every word were being monitored from afar. An electric quiltwork of lights, yellow and blue, mixed with recycled streetlights and an old traffic light or two, revealed the market in splashes of garish color and stark whiteness. Overhead, the lava-forged earth pressed down, cramping the light into a single block of space. An old twinge, a mixture of claustrophobia and vertigo, swept through Manning as he followed Raven to the gunsmith.

There was no mistaking their destination, Manning saw, as they turned the corner into a hollowed cul-de-sac in the tube wall. It was the only shop in the marketplace with a dragon's head mounted above the door, and two antiquated Weatherbees bolted right below in an X pattern. From the size and coloration of the faded scales, it looked like a young drake, probably not more than a few years past full wingspan. Manning thought whoever had taken it was lucky its older partner hadn't flamed them.

"It's a beauty, ain't it?" a voice hollered out from the back of the shop. A gnomish middle-aged woman walked out of the shadows, wiping her callused hands on a faded turquoise rag. The smell of gun oil and soap flared into full strength as she approached. "My husband took that one down in the foothills at the eastern edge of the burn zone. 'Course, after he shot it, he had to chop at the neck for damn near a half-hour to get the head off."

"Where was its partner?" Manning asked. "Only the older, smarter ones ever hunt alone, and that one couldn't have been more than five years past his wings."

"Dragonhunter, eh?" the woman asked. She looked at his duster with a practiced eye. "Must be, to go walking around in something like that. Anyway, Mark said there'd been a group of mountain scavengers, come down into the valley to pick up some salvage. I think he said they'd bagged the older drake, but got fried by this one. He got it as it was heading home. I guess some of them made the old ski resort their nesting ground." Her eyes started to shine. "Hey, you thinking about heading up and taking a shot at their nest? I bet you could bag a shitload." She laughed again, this time at a passing commune dweller who frowned at her language.

Manning smiled in response. "I'm experienced, not crazy. Besides, we're heading elsewhere."

"Fair enough. What can I help you with?"

While Raven watched the shop entrance, Manning and Mrs. Allyn dickered, finally agreeing on a price for the ammunition in dragon scales and other goods they'd picked up in their wanderings. Manning was pleasantly surprised at how fair the final deal was, and made a note to buy from these people the next time he was around. After putting down his initial payment and extracting a promise that the ammo would be ready the next day, he and Raven left the shop and went to make arrangements for lodging. The lights never went down in the underground habitats, but living in the Western Wastes for twenty years had given him a sense of the circadian rhythms better than any atomic clock, and he knew night was approaching.

They settled into a small notch in the Drifter's Hall, rough-hewn but private, and one of the few berths to have a source of running water, a small rivulet bubbling up into a pool that drained back into the wall through the aquifer, and back into the underground river that serviced New Provo. Raven dropped her pack in the corner, furthest from the entrance to the chamber, and filled her washing bowl with water, while Manning sat down and began his nightly ritual of inventorying, inspecting, and cleaning his knives and tools. He took this methodical ritual very seriously; in his mind, it was one of the things that had kept him alive so long. Raven said nothing, listening to the quiet bubbling of their private fountain.

Manning finished his task, and as Raven used their antique camping stove to heat up their canned meals, it struck him suddenly that he would always be alien to her, an exotic visitor from the pre-Change world, doomed to die without seeing it again. On the heels of this insight came the certainty that she would soon strike out on her own. The weight of their difference pressed on him with new force. This world was not safe to be old in.

*   *   *

"How many?" Manning asked Raven as they walked away from the Allyn stronghold, bags heavy with ammo and gun oil. Their followers were waiting two stalls down from the gunsmith, ostensibly buying new blades, but never taking their eyes from Raven.

"Four for sure, possibly a fifth. Two of them got the desert stare," Raven told him sotto voce, without changing expression. She too had been expecting this. "One of them is the young guard at the main gate yesterday."

Manning didn't worry about them getting the better of him and Raven. He had years of experience and still-quick reflexes on his side, and she was a natural warrior. Settlements with ammo and quality supplies were few and far between, however, and he had no wish to be banned permanently from one because some settlers couldn't keep it in their pants.

"Stranger," a voice called out, "how much for the girl? I'm willing to make you a fair offer." The other men snickered, and Manning heard muttering. Resigned to what would happen, he shook his head.

"I'm a free woman," Raven replied without turning around or slowing, "and not for sale. My fate's mine."

"Maybe in the Wastes, you're free," another voice spoke.

"Oh?" Raven said, and stopped walking. Manning stopped as well, and turned around to face the men as she had. There were indeed five, the first being the guard that greeted them at the gate. To Manning, all of them looked desert-stunned, and unwilling to listen. Each carried a gun. *So much for their rules.*

"Your friend can leave, girl," the guard said, casually pointing his pistol at Manning, "but you'll be staying here with us. We need fresh blood in New Provo."

With a blurred flash of steel, Raven uncurled her arm in an underarm throw. Even though he expected it, she moved so suddenly that Manning heard the click of the holster's spring-loader only after the throwing knife was already buried in the guard's eye. His head jerked, spraying blood on the man behind him, and his body flew backwards, landing in a graceless slump of limbs and dust. As Manning watched, the guard's remaining eye seemed to dull as the tube dust settled onto his face, covering him in a pale shroud.

"Happy to oblige," Raven said in the silence.

The other men stood frozen in shock at the sight of their friend lying on the ground. Manning knew this would only last a few seconds. He gauged the distance from where they stood to the gun locker, the main gate, and freedom, and computed the odds that they could run and escape without being shot. Dragonhunters do not survive long by being gamblers, and Manning was better than most. He'd dropped his own throwing knives into position as soon as they'd packed their bags and left the Drifter's Hall.

The oldest of the group looked up, a snarl of rage on his weathered face, and with a snapping motion, Manning buried a blade in his throat. The man dropped his gun, and grabbed the hilt of the dagger. Blood spurted, purple and thick, through his fingers as he tried to dislodge the knife, then pitched forward onto the ground, now spattered with clumps of dirt and blood. Behind him, a man who could have been his younger brother was raising his gun. Manning and Raven threw together, neatly pinning the man's heart and throwing him against the rock wall.

A bullet whined, and Manning heard rock chips spray off the tube wall behind him. Drawing his Bowie knife, he leapt forward in three bounding steps, and drove the blade underneath the sternum and up, burying the eight-inch blade to the hilt in his opponent's chest. He slapped the pistol from the dying man's grip and forcefully pushed him away, pulling the blade free of the falling corpse. A sharp crack rang out, followed by the sound of dead weight hitting the earth. When Manning turned around, he saw Raven brushing off her hands and looking critically at the fifth would-be assailant's body. His head rested at an odd angle on the uneven ground.

"All the fresh blood they could want," Raven whispered in the dusty stillness.

"Yes," Manning agreed. "Let's not wait to see if the people of New Provo want to add ours to it." He shouldered his pack and headed toward the gate. Behind him, Raven went to each corpse and pulled out the blades. They clanked as she deposited them in her drakeskin bag to clean and sharpen later. Long experience taught him that the courage of most vengeful people decreased in direct proportion to the number of fools that he and Raven killed. He knew she would be safe. He was more concerned about getting their guns back.

When he arrived at the gun locker, he was surprised to find their guns lying on the counter. Raven raised an eyebrow, but said nothing. The gates opened as they approached, and they left New Provo as they arrived, on foot and in silence.

Aboveground, the temperature was just short of stifling. Still-blazing rays of yellow heat met them at the marker gate, and Manning was half-tempted to wait in the dark shelter of the rock until nightfall. The thought of being trapped in the gatehouse by a dragon's long flame prompted them to move on. Manning had seen people die that way, and still saw them in his nightmares. Besides, the good people of New Provo might prove him wrong and come out to avenge their own.

Raven scanned the sky quickly, shaking her head at the question in his eyes. He stepped out into the desert's fading light, confirming her scan. Dragons tended not to fly at sunset, for reasons only the damned lizards knew. Apart from very rare exceptions, dragons were daylight creatures, a fact for which Manning was grateful. Dragon eyesight bordered on the supernatural, but didn't seem to include night vision.

Raven checked her gun barrels and clips, disassembling and reassembling the guns with ruthless speed. She looked up at Manning and nodded; the guard had been too busy thinking about his sex drive to bother with sabotage. Manning took a moment to check his weapons as well. He put them away and nodded toward Oregon.

"Westward ho," he said, and began walking. Her footsteps echoed in time with his as they set out, and he wondered how many more times he'd hear that sound.

*   *   *

They were four days past the charred remains of the border rest stop that loomed in a broken jumble at the edge of the Snake River when Manning saw the first glint of sunlight off scales to the east. Like every other day for the past week, the weather was clear and bright, affording plenty of warning before a dragon came within fire range. Manning's biggest fear was a summer thunderstorm, one of those lightning-fraught boomers. Dragons liked to ride the lightning down, and the flashes left afterimages that made the great monsters harder to spot.

"There," he pointed, stopping in the middle of the weed-encrusted road. Raven followed his finger, her eyes narrowing. "Still at least a half-hour off, but closing fast."

"Tracking us?" she asked.

"Maybe. It could have picked up our smell from New Provo. Or it might just be a wanderer, searching for a new clan." He quickly unholstered his rifle. The Oregon countryside was low and hilly, bad for concealment, especially from an aerial attack. *Better to find whatever cover was available and scope out its intentions,* he thought. Raven unslung her binoculars to get a better view. She focused the lenses for a few seconds, and then whispered a curse.

"What?"

"Two. They look like twins from here; they even have the same wing coloration."

"Twins or closely related cousins, then. Shit," Manning swore as he looked around the area. Weeds and wild grass choked the area, which, like most of the broad valley, was nothing but rolling hills and plains. Not even a concrete culvert pipe they could hide in until the dragons headed east to roost. *Probably the worst place to be in for a firefight,* Manning thought. *No cover, and surrounded by fuel. Might as well douse us in barbecue sauce and put up a sign.*

Raven pointed to a slight rise that the road, once part of I-84, cut through and over, making an artificial valley a hundred yards up the road. "Maybe we can crouch down enough to get cover until they're within range."

Manning frowned, but nodded after a second's thought. "Looks like our best bet. Let's take it slow; they might pick us up if we move too fast." Pausing to glance back toward the pair of dragons flying west, Manning turned and began to move toward the hill, modifying his walk to minimize the normal up-and-down gait that dragons could spot so well. Raven followed two steps behind, moving in the same fashion. After an interminable few minutes, they reached the hilltop, and immediately crouched down as low as possible without giving up visual contact.

They watched the dragons for what seemed like an hour, and Manning's heart continued to sink as he watched the dragons' approach with each wingbeat. It was obvious that the dragons weren't flying in their direction on a whim. Whether or not they were actively being hunted he couldn't tell, but he doubted a coincidence. A single dragon may wander from clan to clan; Manning had never seen a pair do so. Unless the entire clan was on the move, dragons rarely strayed from their hunting grounds, which made them easy to find, but difficult to hunt without dying in the process.

Suddenly, when the pair was roughly ten minutes' flight away, the dragons broke out of their side-by-side formation and flew lower, zigging and zagging in a fast-moving pattern. Occasionally, one or the other would spit a white-hot stream of flame, bursting the rich grasslands into combustible life. Soon, the sky was hazy with smoke, and Manning knew the heat from the blaze would be upon them before long.

"They should be within range soon," Raven whispered. "With the sun at our backs, we might be able to surprise them a bit." Her tone was calm, almost cheerful. Manning knew she enjoyed the hunt, even with such odds stacked against them.

"We can only hope. If they get within range, wait until they start the strafing run," he replied. He unslung his rifle and loaded it smoothly, then thumbed the safety off. "A clean shot in the eye will save us firefighting later."

"Agreed," Raven replied. She focused the scope carefully. Still miles away, the dragons looped and soared, now flying in a deceptively slow pattern. Despite how ungainly they looked, dragons could perform maneuvers and accelerate much quicker than any engineer would believe.

One of the dragons fell back and to the left, searing the grass in passing, while the second continued forward, straight toward the hill where Raven and Manning lay in wait. Manning started counting silently. He wanted a clean shot, but not too close to their position. A couple thousand pounds of anything doesn't stop on a dime, especially when flying at attack speed.

Without warning, the lead dragon accelerated, and dove into an unmistakable strafing position: legs drawn up, ears flattened, wings spread to maximum extension. As Manning watched through the scope, the dragon's throat sac, where its natural chemistry lab mixed and stored flammable gases, expanded and retracted in ever-deepening amounts. This one was an older drake, judging from the scars and mottling on the breastplate scales, and had seen a lot of action. Manning lifted the rifle barrel minutely to focus on the dragon's eye. *One round through the old one, and then we can concentrate on Junior.*

"Davis, look," Raven said, shaking his arm lightly and pointing to the northeast. He followed her finger, wondering what had her so agitated, and saw the second dragon, further away than the lead, but also in strafing position. *No wonder she used my first name,* Manning thought.

"Ever seen that before?" she asked him.

"No," he replied, turning back to the senior dragon.

"Great," Raven said, focusing her scope. The dragons were closing in too fast for normal tactics. Setting up crossfire for Junior was out of the question. Despite his fear, Manning almost felt like laughing. A pair of dragons, hunting him and Raven with new tactics, for the first time in the two decades since dragons overran the world, just as she was preparing to leave him behind. It suddenly occurred to Manning that maybe God never left this unhappy world. Maybe He'd just been biding His time, waiting to play a good joke on old Davis Manning.

The lead dragon came within range, throat sac swelled almost to bursting. He'd seen drakes shoot continuous flame for upwards of a minute, which could make even a deeply buried bomb shelter hot enough to melt gun barrels and combust bones. Any poor bastard getting hit with such a flame would be nothing but a shadow scorched into the earth.

Manning fired, aiming for the center of the slitted iris. It seemed to take an eternity for the bullet to strike. Through the scope, he saw the sudden gush of blood, saw the dragon's massive head flinch to the side at the impact. The flinch only lasted for a moment, though, and did not interrupt the flight. Soon, too soon, the dragon raised its head and stared furiously at the hill, at the hunter hiding behind its small rise. With both eyes. Manning's shot had taken it just below the left eye, on a bony ridge that marked the lower edge of the socket. Blood streamed down, but the eye was unaffected.

"Shit," Manning said. He chambered another round, and sighted again. Now, the dragon had almost completely closed its eyes, covering them with heavily scaled lids that were difficult to punch through with anything less than an elephant gun. Only a small swatch of eye was visible as the target loomed closer. The oddsmaker in his brain calmly told him that he had one, perhaps two shots left before the dragon was close enough to roast him.

A roaring scream pierced the air to his left, followed by Raven's muttered "Got you." The smaller drake continued flying, bleeding copiously from one dark ruined eye socket, but staying aloft, increasing its velocity in an effort to reach the hunters before it died. Manning fired, and watched the bullet whine harmlessly off the lower ridge of the dragon's lid. Baring its teeth in response, the dragon seemed to smile. The throat sac expanded, and that same cold voice in his head informed him he had three seconds to live.

"Take the shot, Davis," Raven said, even as she fired into the younger drake's other eye.

Staring through the scope, Manning gently applied pressure to the trigger, but stopped short of the firing point. Inspiration struck, and he abruptly refocused on the dragon's throat sac. Expanded almost to the point of rupture, the scales ruffled like a bird's feathers, standing almost horizontally, and displaying the pale underflesh of the dragon's hide. A sudden memory of watching a cartoon version of *The Hobbit* as a child came to him, and despite the fear in his belly, he smiled briefly.

"Backdraft," Manning said to himself, and fired.

The effect was catastrophic. The sac exploded outward, spreading ragged green-scaled flesh and orange gouts of flame in all directions. Tossed off balance and backwards by the force of the explosion, the drake spun violently to the right, punching one wing into the dirt and nearly ripping it off. Even over the thrumming roar of the explosion, Manning could hear the snapping of the tendons and delicate bones that held the wing together. Blood, so deeply crimson it was nearly black, spewed from the throat and the jagged stump of the dragon's wing.

"Jesus Christ, Davis. What the hell?" Raven whispered in awe as she watched the drake tumble closer in a spray of blood and flesh.

"Surprise," Manning replied distantly. He couldn't take his eyes off the drake, although he already knew it would fall short of their position. Manning felt in his bones that his hatred of dragons would never abate, but watching the pinwheeling corpse of the dragon self-destruct, he felt a trickle of pity for the ravaged, dying beast. Years in the wild had left him with a strong stomach and iron resolve, but now, his stomach turned cold and queasy.

Still tumbling, the drake's neck whipped over in a somersault and plowed into the ground. Dirt erupted, and Manning heard a splintering crack. The body tipped up into the air, momentum nearly spent, and stood on end for an interminable second. Slowly, it fell forward, now entirely dead weight, and crashed into the ground. Dust billowed, then settled around the two hunters, coating them in a silent, powdery haze. Through the gritty film, Manning looked at the drake he'd just killed. Its eyes were open and staring, reminding Manning of the first news broadcasts that announced the Change, the dead and dying scattered in burning streets while the world's new apex predators screeched and battered the skies, so many years and miles ago. As he watched, the ever-present dust began to collect on the drake, covering it in a prelude to Mother Earth's tender loving care. Manning turned away.

Raven looked over at the dragon she had killed, lying still in thick stand of desert grass. Two blasted holes stared out from the younger drake's face; except for those, the dragon looked like it was resting quietly in the late afternoon sunshine. "Mine went down quick and quiet," she said in a mocking tone.

Manning looked over at her kill, then back to his. "Mine went down. We didn't. Tomorrow, that's all that will matter."

*   *   *

Under the bright silver moon, Manning sat next to the fire, holding a leather-bound journal in his hands. Raven slept quietly, untroubled by dreams as far as Manning could tell. For the first time in years, he wasn't sure what he wanted to write. Manning had started his journal a decade prior, after waking up in a Mennonite infirmary that he'd managed to reach after a perilously close encounter with a nestling. He escaped the incident with a badly broken leg, and a compulsion to keep a record of his life.

When he started keeping the journal—writing down names and descriptions of people he'd met, the hunts he'd been on, memories of what life he'd lived before the dragons came—he thought the main purpose was to provide whoever found his corpse with the sum of what he'd learned. Later, he admitted to himself that since he was likely to die in an inferno, keeping such a record would be futile. For years after that, wandering about the Wastes, he'd firmly believed that this journal would be his mark on the world after the dragons were long gone. One man's history of the Dragon Wars.

In the last few years, however, traveling with Raven had shown him the true reason he'd kept the journal, even before he'd known anyone to share with. Watching Raven sleep in the quiet night, he knew it was enough to be commemorated, kept alive in the heart and soul of whoever came after.

Moving silently, he slipped the journal inside Raven's knap-sack and closed the flap. He knew she would leave before he woke up. That was just her way. He looked at her one last time as he settled into his bedroll, seeing her face through the dim flicker of the campfire and the pale moon shadowing.

"Goodbye, Raven," he said softly, and closed his eyes. He fell asleep quickly, and dreamed of rivers flowing gently to the sea, underneath a cloudless, wingless sky.

ALEPH

Grains of snow pelted the dirty window overlooking the city, fulfilling the promise Sergei felt in his ruined knee when he awoke that morning. He shifted his weight in the chair as he waited for the WPA official to finish reading. Across the younger man's desk, folders and forms spilled like water, a puddle of ink and bureaucracy turning slowly into a sea. Sergei thought of a life spent with such forms, filling in check boxes and empty lines, and felt a spark of pity. His career—really, his life—was over, but he had at least tasted glory.

Mr. Lowe sighed, and put Sergei's packet down on the desk. "I'm sorry, Mr. Androv, but I can't put you on this project. This group will be assigned to the Department of the Interior. All of our project workers will be required to hike through national parklands, up to 10 miles a day, and—well, your records indicate … "

Sergei nodded once, sharply. He knew what they said, and besides, the ruined landscape of his knee, the runnels of scar tissue left in the operations' wake, were clear enough. Flashes of muscle memory, the stretch and lift of a flawless plié, shot through him. Did Irena share the same thoughts as she recovered, the pain of a broken floating rib distracting her from the flaw that ended him? She begged his forgiveness in the aftermath, as he lay on the stage, leg afire in the awful moments after his career ended in the snap of a tendon. Sergei had not seen Irena since that night.

"Don't worry, Mr. Androv," the official said, attempting a reassuring smile. "The WPA has a number of projects in the works, and I'm certain we can find one for a man of your talent and obvious fitness." Shutting the folder of Sergei's life, Lowe moved it to the top of a pile that might as well be bound for the incinerator. His pale eyes did not meet Sergei's. "I'll notify you when I have something."

Not when, Sergei thought. *If.* The last of the money from the repertory, an extravagance of guilt on the director's part, was almost gone. How much longer could he wait?

Lowe watched as the former master dancer gained his feet. Echoes of discipline and grace still haunted his movements. Every time he saw Androv, the official wished he had seen the man dance before the accident that ruined him. *He must have been something,* the official thought, as Sergei Androv shook his hand gravely and strode from the office, a slight roll to his right the only sign of injury.

As his eyes roved over the seemingly endless files and folders that buried his desk, Lowe considered Androv's case. Despite what his bosses thought, Lowe tried to find jobs that suited his clients, at least until America recovered and the government didn't have to provide work. Androv was educated, disciplined, and fit, but his dance experience didn't match any of the positions Lowe could legitimately assign to him, and with a ruined leg, he couldn't dance with either of the federally funded troupes. And yet. Chasing a fleeting thought, Lowe opened his desk drawer, and dug through the papers there until he found a thick-stocked business card. He held it up to the light. It was a simple card, the business name embossed in black on the front—Shelman Ironworks—and a telephone number beneath. He wasn't sure he believed what the factory owner had told him, and he knew that many of his clients wouldn't work for this particular employer—the last client he'd tried to refer told him he wouldn't work for a damn Jew, depression or no—but Androv might not be concerned with that, and except for his bad knee, he was exceptionally strong and fit, which is what Mr. Shelman wanted.

He considered the look in Androv's eye, the almost invisible slump in his shoulders as he received the bad news, and Lowe—whose grandfather, decades before, had abbreviated his last name from Lowenski at Ellis Island—knew Androv would take the chance. He picked up the receiver, gave the operator the number, and waited to speak to Mr. Shelman.

*   *   *

February cold skirled around Sergei as he trudged through the gritty courtyard to Shelman Ironworks, a cavernous block of windows and walls at the far end of the 76 line, one stop from where all train trips went to die quietly by the sea. The front doors were open despite the cold, and Sergei felt the tremendous heat of the foundry even before he was inside. A stocky man, thick with muscle, and topped with a threadbare wool beret, waved him over.

"You Androv?" the man asked. Sergei nodded. He heard the thick vowels and muddy rumble of Belarus in the man's voice.

"I'm Konetko. This way." The man led Sergei up a rickety stairway to a dingy office overlooking the ironworks floor. Daylight echoed from the high windows at the far end of the building, but illuminated nothing more than shadows slowly moving around pits of liquid fire and falls of steel. A square man, whose solid head rested on shoulders broad and straight as if cut by a lathe, sat behind an oblong desk. Konetko nodded at the desk, turned, and closed the door behind him as he left.

"Anton Shelman," the boss said, rising to meet Sergei. His handshake was firm and warm. "Mr. Lowe tells me you'd be a good fit for my factory, Mr. Androv. What do you think?"

Surprised by Shelman's directness, Sergei fell back on the truth. "I know nothing of metal work or foundries, Mr. Shelman, but I'm willing to learn if you will teach."

"What do you know of my work here, Mr. Androv?"

Sergei shrugged. "It is an ironworks, a fact I didn't learn until this morning. Mr. Lowe didn't explain his reasoning to me, but ... "

"You trust him."

"I would like to."

"That's something," Shelman said. "Got any problem working for Jews? I'm Jewish, along with most of the management, and about half the floor crew, so if you're an anti-Semite, best keep walking."

"Do you have problems with Russians?" Sergei asked.

Shelman laughed. "You work well, you're my favorite color. Don't give a damn about anything else."

"As long as I have work, I also do not care," Sergei said. "Any man who works is fine with me."

Shelman nodded, looking Sergei up and down. Despite his knee, Sergei maintained his physical discipline, and had the muscled arms and broad torso to prove it. More importantly, Shelman saw, the former dancer was comfortable in his strength, and didn't need to show off.

"When can you start?" Shelman asked.

Sergei took off his coat and rolled up his sleeves.

Shelman laughed. "Let's get you to the floor."

The owner led Sergei down the steps, deeper into the cavernous heat of the works. Sergei felt the sweat break out on his skin, and relished the feeling. It was wonderful to feel sweat that wasn't born of pain or mindless exercise. The men strode past docks and vats and systems that seemed of simple design, but mysterious purpose. Sergei wondered what he could learn of the ways of metal, and why the WPA official thought he would fit in here.

As they entered a long, well-lit locker room, Shelman called, "Vasily!" As the man emerged from the dim, blistering space into the relatively cool room, Sergei was unsurprised to see Konetko coming toward them. In the bright light, Konetko looked even stronger than he had at the foundry's entrance, slabs and cables of muscle moving together in the shape of a man. Konetko lacked the innate grace of a dancer, but he was not clumsy. Sergei guessed he had probably wrestled as a young man, and done well.

The Belarussian stopped, and nodded at Sergei. "He'll be the new driver?"

"That depends on him," Shelman said. "Better show him what he'll be driving."

Konetko rubbed his chin for a moment, looking from Sergei to Shelman, and seemed to come to a decision. "Come on, then," he said with a shrug, "and let's see what you're ready for." He turned and walked back the way he came, Sergei and Shelman following a couple of steps behind.

Sergei carefully navigated a short flight of steps, and followed Konetko to a severe block of steel with an enormous rolling door at the opposite end, large enough to handle a pair of trucks, and maybe a motorcycle between them. His guide paused, withdrew a ring of heavy keys from his pocket, and, choosing a single slender brass key, opened the door onto darkness. He paused halfway through the doorway, and turned to Sergei.

"Do not worry about what you see," Konetko said. "They are inert until activated, and even then, only move when driven or verbally commanded by Rabbi Shelman, who has taken great care to make them so."

"Rabbi?" Sergei said, turning to face Shelman. The religious teacher nodded, his face flushed in the sweltering dimness.

Konetko flipped a heavy switch, activating a bank of actinic white lights overhead. Beneath the lights, arranged in a short block of rows, stood a dozen giant statues, roughly human-shaped, but far larger. Sergei estimated that each was at least nine feet tall. There was little external detail to the statues, except for what looked like handles in the center of each torso, and strangely elongated faces on stumpy heads, which sprang directly from their shoulders. Each statue did have well-articulated hands, arms, and legs, though, which further mystified Sergei.

"Vasily, do we have any that Mr. Androv will fit without redoing the cage?" Shelman asked.

"Two on the far end," Konetko replied, "the ones Jacov and I usually use."

"Good," Shelman said. He gestured for Sergei to wait, and walked to the end of the block, where Konetko had wheeled a small stepladder to the statue at the very end. Shelman quickly climbed the stepladder, took a slip of parchment from his pocket, and opened a compartment Sergei hadn't noticed on the statue's forehead, marked with a letter Sergei recognized as Hebrew. The rabbi slipped the parchment inside, closed the compartment with a pat, and climbed down.

"Do you happen to know any Hebrew, Mr. Androv?" Shelman asked, as he walked back toward Sergei.

"One or two words only," Sergei said.

"Time to learn some more, then," Shelman said. He turned back to the statue and shouted something in Hebrew.

The statue seemed to vibrate for a second, as if it were stiff, and then took a step forward, its foot landing on the depot floor with a thump that shook Sergei. His mouth fell open, but he did not speak, the evidence before his eyes stunning him into silence. The statue took another step, and another, steadily moving toward the side of the depot.

Shelman shouted another command, waving his arm in a "come here" gesture. In response, the statue turned and began walking straight toward the rabbi and Sergei. When it was three steps away, Shelman shouted a third command, and the statue stopped in its tracks and stood before the two men, impassive, and utterly still. Sergei felt no sense of life or animation, but he knew neither his eyes nor his ears had tricked him.

He turned to Shelman, not trying to hide the shock in his face, or the fear in his eyes. "Rabbi, this … this statue is a golem, correct?"

"All of these statues are golems, Mr. Androv," Shelman said, and patted his shoulder. "If I haven't scared you off, you're going to be our new golem driver."

Sergei looked up at the statue, then at the muscular foreman and the foundry owner. If it was a joke, he decided, he would play along, and if it wasn't … well, then, something new was about to enter his life. A spark of excitement ran through him, something he'd almost forgotten. He had no idea how he was to proceed, and the not knowing felt energizing. "How do I begin?"

The first days of his training at Shelman's foundry were both new and familiar to Sergei. He'd been a dancer virtually all his life, training from early childhood at a succession of academies and preparatory schools, so hard work and discipline were old friends. He spent hours learning the operations of the foundry, the terminology of steel, and the steps that took coal and ore heat, and transmuted them into steel, and iron, and other metal products that build worlds. After Sergei's head was stuffed full of concepts and terms, they took him to his training golem, and began the long process of fitting him to his suit.

"Every golem can have a suit plugged into it," Konetko told him as the first leather sleeves were fitted around his limbs, "but the suit itself has to be molded to you. It took us a while to figure that out. There were injuries."

Sergei nodded. He understood the risk, and the toll. Moreover, after his first fitting, he could see where the early problems were. The suit of a golem driver was a series of leather and thin metal sleeves that covered the limbs and torso, and the top half of the driver's head. Each sleeve was connected to a flexible plate, and once placed inside the golem, the plate would make contact with a series of springs and gears. In this way, the driver's movement was transmitted to the golem. Early versions, Konetko told Sergei, were loose, and very flexible. However, if the sleeves slipped, a driver could easily find himself in contact with the machinery within, bruising badly, and even shredding skin and muscle. Shelman developed a more rigid structure for the sleeves, and now injuries from machinery were rare.

"What about heat?" Sergei asked.

"The golems are good insulators," Konetko said. "Not much gets through, but working in there gets hot, so we put a water system in each one."

"I thought golems were made of clay," Sergei said.

"Rabbi Shelman glazes them, inside and out," Konetko said. "Very waterproof."

Konetko's lack of concern comforted Sergei. Not only did Konetko trust in the suits and the golems, he seemed to think Sergei would pick up the necessary skills without coddling, renewing a confidence Sergei hadn't known he'd lost. Now, after the theory and the fittings, he was ready to take his first steps as a golem driver. Or so he thought.

"Relax, Sergei," Shelman told him as he walked across the locker room floor in his suit, testing it for range of motion and comfort. "I'd rather take a few days extra to get you trained up properly than let you out on the floor too soon, and hurt yourself, or someone else. Clay is cheap, and there's plenty of work, even now."

"I understand," Sergei said. He smothered the twinge of disappointment in his chest, knowing that Shelman was wise to insist on training and safety; it made for better work and higher profit in the long run. Still, he'd been a cripple for so long, and while he would never dance again, he had finally begun to believe there was work for him in movement, work that could sustain him. Waiting, even just one more day, when it was nearly upon him, hurt. But Sergei knew how to withstand pain. Another day, and it would be gone.

*   *   *

Konetko hit the lights, filling the locker room with glassy brightness and the monotonous hum of the long tubes overhead. He and Sergei were the first to arrive for the morning shift, and Sergei felt an anxiety in his gut he hadn't experienced for years. Today he would start anew, not just as a steelworker, but as a figure from myth. Today, he was a golem driver.

"Hard work today," Konetko said, the tectonic rumble of his voice cutting through the hum. "Everything you were taught, you relearn, and more. Will your knee hold?"

"Don't expect me to dance," Sergei said.

Konetko laughed. "Maybe a jig, if you get through the day."

Sergei frowned. "A jig? What kind of dance is that?"

"The Irish dance it," Konetko said. "I've seen it done on bars, on doors held up by two men, on tabletops. It's not as complicated as ballet, but you do it fast, and it's something to see. I can do it a little."

"Maybe you should show me," Sergei said, smiling.

"I will make you a deal. You get through the week as a golem driver, and I will teach you what I know of the jig," Konetko said. "Driving the golem is very tough. You're strong, but I don't know if your leg can take it."

"Let's find out," Sergei said. He stood up slowly, the lower half of his driver suit jingling and clinking, and pulled the top of the suit over his shoulders, buckling the thick straps across the broad expanse of his muscular chest. Within a minute, he was fully suited, and he and Konetko walked toward the rolling door at the end of the locker room where their golems awaited. Hooked ladders were attached to each golem, hanging down like phallic parodies. Sergei suppressed a grin as he imagined what they looked like from the far end of the room, and ascended into the golem's open cavity.

"First?" Konetko called from the other golem.

"The Word," Sergei replied, already climbing to the head of the clay statue, a piece of paper in his hand. As he had seen Shelman do that first day, he opened the small compartment built into the golem's forehead, and slipped the paper, which had the word "אמת" scrawled on it in Shelman's rangy hand, into the drawer. The clay began to hum, as if the buzzing of the fluorescents had leaked down and spread throughout its molecules. Sergei lowered himself to the edge of the cavity, adjusted his grip on the handholds built into the top edge of the entrance, and gracefully pivoted his body into place, his legs sliding easily into the tops of the golem's legs. He shifted his weight and checked the connections, making sure everything was locked into place as he'd been trained.

"Next?" Konetko said.

"The Prayer," Sergei said. He didn't see exactly why Shelman called it that, since it had nothing addressed to God. His factory, his rules, Sergei decided, and that was good enough. Shelman had given Sergei a copy of what to say, rendered in phonetic English, but Sergei's memory was excellent, and he'd practiced the harsh Hebrew consonants and liquid vowels until the words flowed smoothly from his lips:

Your will is mine

Your strength is mine

Your movements are mine

We are one

Until released

"Eh, good enough," Konetko said, and laughed. "Button up, and don't forget—"

"—to open the mouth," Sergei finished. "Got it." He reached up and pulled a pair of levers, one of which opened the long vertical drawer of the golem's mouth, the other raising a clear glass shield to protect the operator from sparks and flying metal burrs. Once the shield was in place, he closed the doors to the golem's trunk, and latched them in place. Now, Sergei knew, between the water system inside the golem, and the tremendous heat resistance of its body, he was completely protected from burning, as long as he didn't decide to take a swim in the molten steel vats.

"Can you hear me?" Konetko asked, his voice carrying clearly through the acoustic tubes into Sergei's ears. In response, Sergei slid his arms into the golem's empty limbs, locked the sleeves into place with a few twists, and gave Konetko a thumbs-up, the golem's hand and arm responding as easily as his own. Konetko nodded, making the entire golem shake up and down in a series of staccato bows.

"Now, the Work," Sergei said, and began to move. Beneath him, the golem's legs rocked the body back and forth, balancing on one ponderous foot, then the other. There was a sense of heaviness, of geologic power stored within, but no drag or burden the former dancer could feel. Inside his own golem, Konetko lifted his arm in a sweeping gesture directed at the great rolling door.

"Lead the way," he said.

Carefully, each step sending rolling vibrations up into his legs, Sergei walked out of the locker room onto the foundry floor. Konetko followed at his shoulder, waiting to see if Sergei remembered where to go. Without hesitating, Sergei strode across open space, heading toward the pour station that Konetko and Shelman assigned him that morning. Eventually, Shelman told Sergei, he would be trained on every station, but pouring was always the first, as it was the simplest in the ironworks.

"The rabbi has a large contract with the Navy," Konetko said as Sergei reached the molds. "Lots of large pieces, but pretty standard shapes. You'll be pouring for a while. Ready?"

"Yes," Sergei said. He felt strong, but jittery, just as he had before every one of his performances. Alive.

"OK," Konetko said. "You're on the clock." A piercing whistle blasted throughout the foundry. Shift start. Sergei turned to the first mold, and a vat of molten steel waiting for him to pour.

*   *   *

By the end of the first day, Sergei estimated he'd guzzled two gallons of water over the course of his shift. As Konetko had told him, the glazed golem kept out the punishing heat, but his own exertions generated enough that he was hard-pressed to tell the difference, even with the regular spray of cooling mist. His clothes were stiff from repeated soaking and drying, as were his muscles from the labor of pouring steel and maneuvering the heavy vats and molds, and the tension of driving the golem with both his will and body. When the whistle blew at shift end, Sergei stretched his arms and back, deeply satisfied with the day's labor.

Despite 30 minutes of stretching and calisthenics when he got home, and a long shower as hot as he could stand, he still woke up sore, slabs of tightness across his back and thighs, reminding him that this work was new to him. Now, though, Sergei knew what to expect, and had a better idea of how to avoid some of his mistakes of the previous day.

The labor was hard, even with the golem's power, but Sergei drank it all in. Marveling at work he'd never before even dreamed of, absorbed in the details and broad strokes of his tasks, the days skipped past in a glow of sweat and manual labor. He'd finished the last pour of a support beam mold, and was preparing for another, when the shift whistle blew, and Konetko clapped him on the shoulder.

"Time for the weekend," he said.

"Weekend?" Sergei said.

"Tomorrow is the Sabbath for Jews," Konetko replied, "and the others take Sunday as the Sabbath, so we don't work either day. Rabbi doesn't seem to mind. We get enough work done during the week, he says."

"Good," Sergei said. "I could use the rest."

Konetko laughed. "Get changed, and we'll go have a drink. I have a present for you."

Sergei nodded, bowing up and down quickly, and headed across the floor, waving to three other golem drivers as he did, and watching around him for careless pedestrians. Nobody had suffered an accident in Shelman's ironworks for months, but Sergei didn't want to be the one to break that streak. He respected the power he held when driving the golem.

After parking the golem in place, and deftly unseating his suit from the gears and levers, Sergei opened the front hatch, climbed up onto the cavity and opened the golem's forehead. He withdrew the scrap of paper within, and closed the drawer, feeling the anima leave the glazed clay under his hands. Inscribed on the drawer was the Hebrew letter he'd noticed the first day he'd seen the golem: א. Sergei now knew it was *aleph*, the first letter of the Hebrew alphabet.

"The first," Sergei said aloud. "Where things start." He liked the sound of that.

Outside the cavernous ironworks, February showed no sign of releasing its grip. Despite being on his feet all day, lifting and pushing and moving, Sergei's knee felt good, so he knew no new snow would fall that night. Pulling his coat open to let the chill cool him, Sergei walked four blocks toward the city, and turned down a short bump of stairs. The Red Dog had been a speakeasy just a few years prior, but became a workingman's bar when Prohibition ended, and now served mostly steelworkers and Teamsters.

A blast of warmth, smelling of beer and sweat, met Sergei when he opened the door. He stepped inside and waited for his eyes to adjust, then looked around the crowded bar and floor space, stuffed with tables, and men talking, laughing, and raising a glass to payday. He saw Konetko and a couple of others from the ironworks at the end of the bar, and walked toward them, skirting the low-hanging lamps and rough-hewn tables.

To his surprise, Mr. Lowe from the WPA was among the men at the bar, drinking from a mug that looked as big as his head. Sergei offered his hand, glad to have a chance to show his gratitude.

"Vasily tells me you're fitting right in, Mr. Androv," Lowe said over the laughter and ruckus. His handshake was firm and confident, stronger than Sergei remembered.

"I'm glad he thinks so," Sergei said. "Thank you for the chance, Mr. Lowe. It's a good job, and I'm grateful."

Lowe smiled. "You're welcome, and call me Abe."

"Hey, Androv," Konetko said, "I told you I'd teach you how to do a jig, so watch."

Moving quickly despite his size, Konetko vaulted onto the bar and spun to face the open floor. The ceiling arched surprisingly high for a basement, leaving plenty of room for the Belarussian. His friends started clapping, keeping a simple beat, and Konetko began to dance. He kicked and spun, his legs moving but his trunk staying still, and Sergei was surprised at Vasily's agility. It wasn't a complicated dance, but it took concentration and fluidity, more than Sergei expected to see. He paid attention to Konetko's steps, noting the pattern and number of moves, and thought that maybe, this was one dance he could manage. His feet started to count the beat, shuffling side to side as he rolled his shoulders in time, mimicking Konetko's dance.

"What the hell," Sergei said in his native Russian, and came to a decision.

Later that night, as he stumbled onto a lonely subway platform after two or three too many beers, Abraham Lowe would marvel at his good fortune. Not only had he successfully placed a man in a job that might give him a new career, he'd had the unmistakable pleasure of seeing two men, bound by common labor, dancing a riotous jig on a battered bar, while longshoremen and steelworkers roared their approval. He hadn't seen a crippled former dancer, or a wrestler past his prime, but two steelworkers enjoying a Friday night, in good health and with time on their side. *Somewhere,* he thought with a laugh, *my rabbi grandfather is smiling at what the golems hath wrought.*

OPERIS DIGNITATE

Sleek and dark, the elevator descended smoothly. Father Albert Carrera, already chilled by the server farm's air conditioning, repressed a shiver and composed his face. Years ago, shortly after his ordination, he had hoped to work at Castel Gandolfo some- day, helping in the Holy See's mission of studying the heavens. That hope was dashed, he knew. His transgressions made sure of that.

"Our mission here is simple, Father," his guide and eleva- tor companion said. Little was known of Cardinal Rambozo's recent years, but fraternal gossip held that Rambozo had been on the bleeding edge of quantum computing research. Carrera possessed thorough grounding in mathematics and astrophys- ics, but what he'd read of Rambozo's published work might have been written in Sanskrit by a drunk for all he'd understood.

"I'm told the focus is cryptographic research," Carrera said.

Rambozo smiled, a grim slash on his haggard face. "In a sense. More accurately, the research is a beneficial consequence of its main purpose."

The elevator stopped. Rambozo pressed a long finger to the elevator's touchscreen control, and HOLD flashed white against a crimson background. The cardinal turned to face Carrera directly.

"I am aware of your previous troubles, Father Carrera. The Lord may judge you, but that is His prerogative and His alone. However, given the ... nature of those troubles, it's important I be assured of your self-discipline and restraint."

Carrera met the cardinal's gaze, clenching his jaw against the rush of shame. "Your doubts are reasonable, Cardinal. Despite my failings, I have not forgotten my training. I am humbled and repentant, and ask only that I be allowed to demonstrate my resolve."

Rambozo regarded the younger man for a moment. His unblinking gaze enveloped Carrera. Whatever the cardinal saw seemed to satisfy him. "A demonstration. Indeed."

With a flick of his fingers, Rambozo released the hold, and the elevator doors opened. The cardinal and the priest stepped into a circular foyer of stone walls hung with modern abstract art, a slab of steel and polarized glass directly opposite them. An HD monitor screen was mounted at eye level to the right of the door, showing a room full of empty cubicles with computer screens and medical gear in each. A biometric scanner rested below the monitor.

"Do the researchers keep business hours?" Carrera asked.

Rambozo shook his head. "No, we're staffed at all hours. The data sets involved are tremendous in size, and the cryptographic analysis never stops."

"Where are they?"

"Go inside and see." Rambozo pressed his hand to the plate, which quickly turned green. The massive door opened, and

Rambozo motioned Carrera inside. The younger man walked through, and found himself inside a security cage. Beyond the enclosure, cubicles bracketed the cage on two sides, separated by an enclosed passage that led to a center control room. Every cubicle had a person inside, typing or manipulating shapes on the screens before them. Every person wore a face mask connected to medical equipment that held cylinders. Every cylinder was filled with something dark and red.

"Cardinal?" Carrera said. "Who are these people?"

"They're obsessive to an astonishing degree," Rambozo said, gazing across the chamber. No one looked up from their tasks. "Puzzle solvers, every single one. There's normal variation in intelligence, but even the least gifted of them can perform more in-depth pattern recognition and analysis than a supercomputer."

"I don't understand. What is the purpose of the equipment?" Carrera asked.

"That's how we feed them," Rambozo said. "Obviously, we can't allow them to hunt."

"Hunt...what?" Carrera said.

"Us, if they get out," Rambozo said, a hint of a smile in his voice. "You've noticed the lack of iconography on the walls?"

Carrera hadn't, but a quick look around confirmed there were no crucifixes or icons within sight. He'd thought the directions to leave all trappings of his office behind—rosary, crucifix, Roman collar—were a reflection of his sins. Now they made a different kind of sense.

"Any symbol of our Lord and Savior carries power they cannot abide," Rambozo said.

Carrera was no fool. The conclusion he was meant to draw was obvious, even to someone only familiar with Hollywood depictions. What was unclear was the reasoning behind Rambozo's charade.

"This is a lot of effort for a joke, even a nonsensical one," Carrera said. The muscles along his jaw flexed as he tried to keep his voice neutral. "I understand that my sins—"

"If this were a joke, you would be correct," Rambozo said. "You are intelligent, and trained in the ways of analysis and logic. If this were normal human endeavor, you'd be well suited for a researcher position. Here, however, you have another qualification: you are defiled. Normally, you would have been—should have been—defrocked and turned over to secular authorities."

Rambozo gestured to a place near the far wall in the second row of cubicles. Carrera stepped forward to follow the cardinal's gesture. He scanned the row.

An empty cubicle.

Behind him, a heavy slam. Carrera turned to see a solid meshwork of steel separating him from the cardinal. Rambozo watched him, unblinking.

"As it happens, even the undead can die. We had an opening, and though you have profaned your holy orders, you can still serve God in a way."

An electronic lock clicked, the vibration running through Carrera's hands as he clenched the meshwork. Rambozo turned his gaze outward.

"Very little can shake them from their puzzles once engaged, but the smell of fresh human and the sound of locks opening tends to work." Though Rambozo's stare was flinty, Carrera saw a glimmer of sympathy. Over the pounding of his blood, Carrera heard the shuffle of feet around him.

"I will pray for you, Father," Rambozo said.

Cold, fetid breath played across Carrera's neck.

"They will show you what to do when you rise," Rambozo said. "Get to work."

ONE FOR THE ROAD

"You don't need me anymore," Rafe told David. The two sat together on a picnic table in a tree-stuffed park, their feet resting on the splintered bench. Over the immense canopy, a brilliant half-moon glittered, scattering sheaves of light through the leaves, and mottling all the shadows with flashes of silver. A squirming form lay on the ground next to the table, wrapped under hulking chains. Low snarls and moans escaped its mouth, but nothing that worried either man. It was just a ghoul, and a fairly young one, or it wouldn't have fallen for the old "lost at night" trick. Only fire, and a lot of it, could take down an old ghoul, but there weren't any around anymore.

"Come on, Rafe." David took a bite of his sandwich. Roast beef on wheat, with Swiss cheese and tomato, and slathered with brown mustard. The smell brought a hungry moan from the ghoul. Ghouls loved brown mustard; that's why David had chosen it. That, and he loved it, too. "How can you even think of breaking up the band?"

"Even the Beatles had to call it quits." Rafe popped the last bite of his sandwich in his mouth. Pastrami, onion, cheddar, a touch of vinegar, and a ghoul's favorite condiment. Great sandwich. Torturing a ghoul was a bonus. "Plus, I'm not much of a hunter anymore. Don't waste your breath; you've been carrying my water for a long time now."

"Rafe, you're a better hunter asleep than anybody else awake," David said through a mouthful of food. He swallowed and spoke again. "Even if all you do is support work, you're still an asset. Besides, who's better than us?"

"Who besides us is still doing this shit?" Rafe asked. "Everybody I know died or quit. Mostly died. Besides, we won. We worked ourselves out of a job, buddy. Werewolves been gone for decades, all the witches and warlocks too, and you and me took out the last vampires."

"Sticks," David said with a smile. "What a bastard. Detroit, right?"

"Nah, Lansing. The Duke and that half-zombie he made, trying to create a new bloodsucker," Rafe said. "That was Detroit."

"Oh, yeah," David said. "All right, so we got the big bad asses. Don't you think there's plenty of cleanup? Hell, we just found this guy."

"Might have to throw this one back," Rafe said. He slid down to the bench and swatted the ghoul in the head. It snapped its jaws at him, but without enthusiasm. Ghouls weren't the sharpest knives in the nocturnal bestiary, but this one was quick enough to know its time was drawing near. As far as Rafe was concerned, the real problem with ghouls, besides their diet, was they had no guts. Catch a vampire, you had a fight on your hands. Werewolves were infamous for ferocity, and magic slingers … taking down one of those earned your own epic song. Ghouls just didn't create much ruckus.

A hunter had to stumble into a nest to get much out of them. Killing ghouls was like stomping bugs.

"We can't have got 'em all," David said.

"All the ones fit to kill," Rafe said. "There might be a few human-monster hybrids still running around, but those keep to themselves. The real nightmare citizens – demons, their offspring, every one of the ferocious and primal beasts – they're all pooched."

Rafe sat back and took a deep swallow of Coke. All things considered, he'd prefer a Bud, but no drinking until the monster was ash. Since the night he and Snyder had found David – the night Snyder bought it in a drab, plastered hallway – Rafe avoided beer and booze until the hunt was finished, and something was burning. In his wolf hour thoughts, he sometimes wondered if the Dutch courage they'd had that night is what got his partner killed. Snyder had been just a hair too slow in dodging the kick that erased his skull. Was it the shots? Rafe didn't think so. Most of the time.

"So, it gets tougher to find things," David said. "That's what makes it hunting."

"We call it hunting because killing makes it sound wrong," Rafe said, and slid off the bench, landing right next to the ghoul. It didn't snap at him, and a twinge of disappointment shot through Rafe. No damn gumption at all. Putting a bullet in its head and lighting it up would be just another chore, like taking out the trash or painting the house. Not that he knew what that was like.

"Ah," David said, still perched on the table. "You're tired of killing shit."

"Well, yeah," Rafe said. "Aren't you?"

"If I thought there was nothing left to kill, yeah, but there's still monsters out there, even if they're not the big evils we used to hunt. It's not over."

Rafe sighed. "I've put in enough blood, and paid my way out of this shit plenty."

David jumped to his feet, arching his body over the bench and the ghoul with a grace Rafe couldn't match, now or ever. In a way, Rafe was grateful for that. The price of that grace was far too high; memories of his parents didn't end in blood like David's did.

"Damn it, Rafe, I'm asking you; hell, I'm begging you," David said. "Don't throw in the towel yet. Let's pop this trash and head south, through Arizona. I've been hearing rumors of something going around near the Navajo lands. Maybe it's a lizard dude, or a skinwalker. Give it one more shot. I ain't ready for this to be a one-man show."

Rafe looked his friend in the eye, put a hand on his shoulder. "David, I didn't just have this idea yesterday. More than twenty years, I've been hunting and killing all the things that would make smart people, sane people, run like hell if they knew about them. I'm tired of killing nightmares; goddamn, am I tired of it. This fucker here is the end of the line."

A moment of silence passed between them. David held Rafe's gaze with a steady glare, and Rafe prepared to get hit; David didn't have a temper, but this was the angriest he'd seen his friend in a long time. If David punched him, there was a fair chance he wasn't getting up soon, or at all. David was the secret weapon of the hunter fraternity, a mutant who, due to some quirk in his family line, was able to take on virtually anything they'd ever hunted. Nobody Rafe had ever known, even doctors and researchers, could explain David's abilities to Rafe's satisfaction. Rafe had seen him throw punches that could dent steel plate and splinter solid oak pillars, move faster than thought, and count the hairs on a fruit bat winging through a moonless night. Against power like that, Rafe knew his scarred and weathered face would disintegrate like smoke. Like Snyder's head had disintegrated under a vampiric kick, like his mentor Simone had splattered under a boulder thrown by an osteovore, like his first partner had been shredded by a pair of zombies in a Georgia pine grove, like any of a hundred other friends and partners he'd lost over the years. Blood, pain, and a brain full of bad memories. He'd paid enough.

A shadow passed over David's face, and the fight dropped out of him. His expression tilted over into sad, and Rafe knew his friend was letting him go. Part of him rejoiced, even as another part, the shadow that roared and drove the hunt inside him, withered and fell into nothing. Rafe knew his decision was right. He also knew turning away from this would kill something he'd relied on all his life.

"Before you go," David said, a tremor barely hidden, "we should take care of this corpse eater. One for the road."

Both men looked down at the ghoul, still chained at their feet. It hadn't even stirred, hoping the hunters would forget about it in the moment. Under their gaze, the oversized eyes, flesh-pale in the shadows, wilted and dimmed. Its long bloodless body, all angles and bones and mottled skin, curled into an ugly parody of sleep.

David squatted down, grabbed a handful of chain and, with a sweeping overhand motion, slung the bound ghoul into the fire pit the men had deepened earlier. The pit would never be fit for use again, but that wasn't their concern. Odds were, nobody would come close enough to this particular site anyway, and even if they did, the ghoul's death residue would scare people away at a subconscious level. *In willful blindness is the preservation of the world,* Rafe thought sourly, and picked up the gasoline jug from its resting place under the picnic table.

"I can't believe it didn't smell the gas," David said as they walked toward the pit. "Aren't they supposed to have super-smell?"

"They used to," Rafe said absently. "This one's not old enough for that to kick in."

"Never will be," David said. They reached the edge of the fire pit and looked down. If the ghoul had moved from where it landed, they couldn't tell. Even David's night vision couldn't catch a trace of movement or interest. Its eyes were closed, and gave no sign it noticed them. Rafe opened the cap and began splashing the ghoul with unleaded. It didn't move then either.

"Light it up," Rafe said as he poured the last of the gasoline out, leaving the ghoul lying in a pool that gathered faster than the ashen ground could absorb, "and step the hell back."

"Ahead of you," David said from ten feet behind him. Rafe heard the sound of a match striking, and jumped back. A point of fire tumbled through the air, and Rafe shaded his eyes. A flash erupted, sending a pillar of flame toward the moon, and still the ghoul made no sound. The men stood there, watching the monster burn and crackle, unmoving until the first hints of dawn began to play through the trees. No sound issued from the pit, or from either man, and though they drove back to town together, they did not speak again. Not even to say goodbye.

IN THE FORESTS AND THE WILDS

Dee felt the boards of her front porch creak through her soles, and had the .45 in hand before the first knock sounded. It had been a long time coming, and she wasn't sure if maybe she didn't deserve it after all, but that didn't mean she would let it happen. Whatever brought her down would have a souvenir to remember Dee Luna by.

She waited silently by the door. Another knock, heavy against oaken planks.

"You're standing by the door, Luna. I can smell the gun oil." The voice was amused, soft and genderless. Dee knew she'd heard it before, but she'd heard a lot of voices. She thumbed the hammer back, letting the click fill the air.

"There's no fight here. I came to offer you something, if you want it," the voice said, still amused, but more serious this time. Dee heard what was under the words. She'd heard it in her own voice often enough, trying to talk something down from a rampage, trying to keep someone from letting their inner beast loose. It hardly ever worked. Still, she'd been an optimist for so long. The habit, she was surprised to find, was tough to lose.

"Please, Luna. I mean you no harm. I swear by the Power," the voice said quietly. Recognition flooded Dee's brain, and her eyebrows arched. This one probably meant it, because if it hadn't, nothing Dee had worked into the cabin's defenses would have stopped it from crashing in. Dee swung open the door, revolver still in hand, ready to fire.

The face and body were unfamiliar to Dee, but the eyes, sharp and green, with flecks of silver scattered through the irises like refugee stars, gave it away. They always did. Never could hide the eyes, no matter the face that held them.

"Hello," the shapeshifter said.

*   *   *

Inside the blind, Dee waited, her clothes covered in mud and brush to mask her scent. Eyes shaded by a wide-brimmed hat, she scanned the woods in the purple, pre-dawn murk. The woods were quiet, but Dee knew the forest could be silent as a tomb and she would still miss what she sought. Even paranoids miss things; that shapeshifter who'd visited her the year before reached her porch before she'd even known it was there.

Patiently, she waited. This wasn't her first hunt.

Sunrise slowly turned the world brighter, and with the light came movement and sound. Wings fluttered, squeaks and cries echoed. If she concentrated, she could almost feel the insect world move around her, hear the tiny rumblings of worms in the dark soil beneath. Despite being no more than a five-mile hike from a busy highway and national park, this part of the forest might have been forgotten by man. In that moment, Dee loved the world.

And then, she saw it. Nearly nine feet tall, slabs of muscle and sinew barely disguised by the rolling expanse of coarse fur. She wanted to put her eye to the scope of her rifle, get a better view, but any movement, even a stray crumb of excitement, could warn it, cause it to go dim and vanish into the shadows. So, she waited.

The creature most knew as Sasquatch made its way through the underbrush, walking southeast alongside a trickle of creek upwind of her, into older clumps of fir and pine. It moved calmly but with purpose, strolling across the woody, uneven terrain as if moving along a sidewalk. Even her people had trouble tracking a Sasquatch that wanted to remain invisible. This was only the second one Dee had ever seen herself. A tremor passed through her, and Dee understood, maybe for the first time, what "awesome" truly meant.

She watched it move through the morning, admiring its grace and power. Her modified .30/06 rested in the crook of her arm as she regarded what she'd come to find. There it was, out looking for breakfast, without a care in the world.

The wind whispered to her, and from the north, she heard the low cacophony of two people trying for silence by walking slowly. Compared to the grace or harmony of a Sasquatch, they sounded like an elephant stampede. The Sasquatch stopped and turned its massive-browed head toward the sound, but didn't fade. It simply waited.

The footsteps came closer, and with them, another sound, a low humming that rolled like hornets on the move, but more subdued. Slowly, carefully, Dee leaned forward and looked up and out into the upper halves of the trees. A small drone hovered just above the foliage line, its camera trained on the creature.

Those cheating bastards, Dee thought.

*   *   *

Against every instinct and Dee's good sense, she had let the shapeshifter in. She even offered it tea.

Sitting across the plain table, Dee imagined all the things her father and older brother would say if they saw her now. Of all the things they had ever hunted in generations of thinning the cryptid ranks, shapeshifters were among the worst. Clever, ruthless, stronger than humans to a ridiculous degree, and seemingly immune to time, they were hard to kill and difficult to discover. The memory of her family's voices weighed on her, demanded violence.

Dee looked at the shapeshifter, and realized it could read the struggle in her face. It nodded, smiling.

"So," Dee said. "Why haven't I killed you yet?"

"You're intrigued, I imagine," it said. "You know what I am, and I know what you can do. If it came down to a fight, there is enough uncertainty about the outcome that I wouldn't make any bets."

"Flatterer," Dee said.

"Even so," it said. "The fact is, we need you. There's a job that needs to be done, and you're uniquely qualified. One might call it kismet."

Dee snorted, and took a drink of her tea. It was slightly peppery, and stung pleasantly going down. "There's no shortage of killers around."

The shapeshifter put its mug down on the smooth tabletop and met Dee's gaze. To her surprise, it seemed concerned, and a little disappointed. "I'm going to run a hypothetical by you. I'd like you to tell me how close I am to the truth."

Dee nodded.

"OK. Most days, when you wake up, you feel heavy, as though your body were thinly coated in lead, like you're moving through syrup all the time. Your doctors, if you've seen any, think it might be depression, or fibromyalgia, or some other ailment that's tough to pin down, but easy to prescribe for, but none of that helps. The only thing that does help is water. When you step into a creek or river, or when you're out in the rain, you feel normal again, like you've regained your strength, your color. When the rain stops, or when you get back to land and dry off, you're back to struggling though a muted world."

The shapeshifter looked at Dee, waiting. From the living room, the ticking of the end-table clock echoed in the stillness. Dee's jaw muscles slackened in shock.

"That's what I thought," it said. "Hoped for, actually. You can help us."

"What is going on?" Dee asked. Part of her couldn't believe she was talking to a shapeshifter, much less asking one for advice, but Dee prided herself on being pragmatic. Know the terrain before you track.

It shrugged. "Well, you're a victim of your own success. You and your people managed to hunt the nocturnal bestiary into near-extinction, so as we went underground, you weren't exposed to us anymore. But between the abilities passed down to you over generations, and the constant exposure to creatures of magic, you've been enveloped in low levels of magical energy all your life. Until now, when the remnants of my people have fled underground. Since you're the last of your kind, it's like you went cold turkey."

Dee blinked. She thought for a moment, and blinked again. "Are you saying I'm going through withdrawals?"

The shapeshifter laughed once, a rueful sound in Dee's cozy dining room. "Good as any diagnosis, I guess. I think it's more accurate to say you have magical poisoning, like getting a high dose of radioactivity. Something in the hunter genome might have counteracted the magical energy when there were enough of you, or enough of us. That's gone now, though."

Dee cocked her eyebrow. She wanted to say it sounded like bullshit, but it fit. Damned if it didn't. "So why do you care?"

"The last hunter of my people dying out? I don't," it said. "But I do care about my people. There aren't a lot of us left, but we could make a life for ourselves if we had somewhere safe, far away from humanity." It leaned forward in its chair, focusing its starlight eyes on Dee's. "We have a refuge, a hidden place between the walls of reality. Just because it's hidden doesn't mean it can't be found, though."

"Close the gate behind you," Dee said. "Can't imagine there's much of anything here you'd miss."

"Wi-Fi is nice," the shapeshifter said. "And pizza. I would miss pizza. Doesn't matter, though; for this place to exist, it needs to be anchored here. Don't ask me why," the shapeshifter said, holding its hands up in a warding gesture. "I didn't write the old magic; I just live with it."

"Fine," Dee said. "What's this got to do with me?"

"Every gate needs a gatekeeper," the shapeshifter said. "We want you to be ours."

*   *   *

Dee had no respect for hunters who went after their prey with gadgets and technology, but whoever was flying the drone moved with precision and finesse, keeping the Sasquatch easily within sight as it moved through the forest. Surely the Sasquatch heard the drone, but Dee understood it might not know what it was hearing. It certainly didn't seem to fear it, or the two people Dee heard bumbling through the woods toward them.

The drone dipped, and Dee noted the stubby cylinder underneath its body just as a flat firing sound reached her ears. The Sasquatch seemed to twitch, and a mild grunt escaped its mouth. Her teeth gritted in fury. *They tagged the damn thing,* Dee thought. She wrapped her hand around the rifle's stock.

With a thudding crash, the two so-called hunters came into view, dressed in forest camo and goggles. Their vest pockets were stuffed with gear, and both men had cellphones on hip-mounted clips. The taller of the two had a tablet in his hands, guiding the drone overhead. He looked up from his screen and gasped, then both men froze as they spotted the Sasquatch, who continued moving through the woods without concern. Dee carefully readjusted her position and brought the rifle into position, ready for sighting. Only the Sasquatch seemed to be relaxed as it trudged along its forest path. Dee wondered what it was thinking, then wondered if it knew what she was thinking. *Wouldn't that be about right,* she thought.

"Holy shit," the shorter hunter stage-whispered. "We found it."

"And tagged it," the drone pilot stage-whispered back. "Look, showing up strong. We could follow it to Canada." The drone pilot tapped his screen and smiled.

Dee put the rifle to her shoulder and lined up her shot. At this distance, a scope would just be overkill. She nestled the stock further into her shoulder. She decided to shoot the drone pilot first. He might not be the leader of this trip, but he was the one obviously cheating. No honor in his hunt.

She exhaled slowly and squeezed the trigger, feeling the lighter kick against her muscles. The tranq dart whuffed out of the barrel and hit the drone pilot near the base of his collarbone. Before he could say, "Ow, shit," she'd fired another dart, striking his companion in the shoulder. A friend in the veterinary profession had been kind enough to tell her about a ketamine derivative that could put down anything from foxes to rhinos. Both men fell unconscious within seconds. The Sasquatch took little notice, idly picking a bit of bark from the nearest tree.

Carefully, Dee climbed out of the blind and made her way to the sleeping hunters. She checked their breathing, searched through their wallets, and confiscated their phones and tablet. She landed the drone, and turned around to face the Sasquatch, who had silently moved beside her while she worked. *Awful lot of muscle to be moving that quietly*, she thought.

"You know who I am," she said to the Sasquatch. "What I do." The Sasquatch nodded.

"Were you in on the plan?" Dee asked.

The Sasquatch gazed at her calmly. It didn't seem to be concerned with her questions, or her unconscious prey.

Then she got it.

"You were observing me," Dee said. "Wanted to see what I'd do?"

It stared at her a moment more, then inclined its head.

"Did that shapeshifting bitch know?" Dee asked.

A moment of silence, then the Sasquatch threw back its head and roared. Dee started, until the Sasquatch put both hands to its belly and roared again, even louder than before. The hunters didn't stir at all.

Goddamn laughing Sasquatch, she thought.

Dee reached up as far as she could, grasped the tip of the tracking dart, and yanked it out of the Sasquatch's shoulder. If it felt the dart go, it gave no sign, just continued to laugh. She held it up to the Sasquatch's face.

"Be more careful, please," she said. "These assholes and their toys."

The reply in the Sasquatch's eyes couldn't have been clearer if he'd spoken aloud.

Like you?

Dee grumbled, and put the dart in a pouch on her belt. She'd dispose of it later. One of the hunters stirred, and she turned to make sure he wasn't coming out of it. When she turned back, the Sasquatch was gone.

*   *   *

"Thanks for your help," Dee said, as they drove away from the parking lot of Kitty's Lounge. In the back corner of the parking lot, two unconscious men lolled in the front seat of a newish SUV. When they finally awoke, they would find themselves without wallets, phones, gadgets, or pants. More importantly, they would also be missing any memory of the last few days and the general purpose of their trip, thanks to one of the residents of the preserve. *The ketamine might have had something to do with it, too,* she reflected.

"Glad to help," the shapeshifter said. "You look better, by the way."

Dee turned to look at her passenger, but saw nothing in its face but honesty. She sighed. Trying to outguess a shapeshifter was tougher than just taking it at face value. "I feel better. I can tell the preserve is draining the residual magic from me. I feel like myself again."

"Good," it said. "Purpose probably helps."

"Probably," Dee said. "Speaking of purpose, why me? What made you think I would be the right person for this?"

The shapeshifter sat back in the passenger seat, thinking. Its eyes twinkled, emeralds and diamonds in its shadows. "At the cabin, you said that there were plenty of killers around. You said 'killer,' but you said it like 'murderer.' They're not the same. Hunters, for example, kill for food or protection. Murderers kill because they can. Not all of my people understand that distinction, but I do. So do you. That's why."

The shapeshifter paused. "Plus, I thought I had you over a barrel with the magical poisoning thing."

Dee laughed, long and loud, and the hunter and the shapeshifter drove away from humanity, back into the depths of the forest, and the world kept secret within. Home.

THE NIGHT MAIL

S unset bloodied the sky before Isaac was ready to get up. A *nar-cocorrido* echoed up the concrete stairwell outside his front door, telling the story of a drug mule turned fertilizer somewhere along the Rio Grande. Isaac sat up from his rat's nest of bedding, a solid, brown, half-Cherokee mass of muscle, and looked out the one decent window in his little apartment. It faced west, the land of promise and day's end, toward the empty spaces of his usual work. *Go west, young man,* he thought. Lately, he'd been going as far as Pendleton, doing his best to stay invisible out there. Meth traffic had picked up out by Umatilla, and the cops were out as much as they could afford.

A short blast of electric guitar sounded from his night stand, the opening riff to Iron Maiden's "The Number of the Beast." Isaac flipped open the phone and held it to his ear. "Yeah."

"Hope you got a clean pair of underwear, Ice," Half Smith said.

"Portland?" Isaac asked.

"Wrong way," Half Smith said. "Tremonton."

"Where the fuck's that?" Isaac pulled a pair of jeans up over his hips. He felt like he should be smoking, even though he'd kicked the habit years before. Talking to a crime boss felt like something that should be done with cigarette in mouth. A Camel, maybe, or a Lucky Strike. "Or is that somebody's name?"

"Tremonton, Utah. You're dropping something off. No pickup. Probably eight, nine hours round trip. Maybe you want to spend the night somewhere."

"All right. That long on the road, I'm gonna need something with leg room and nice seats."

Half Smith chuckled. "Got just the thing. Nice radio too. Shame there's fuck all for stations out there."

Isaac grunted in response, thinking about a night on the road. He loved driving, loved the sensation of passing by unseen while all the daylight people slept away the darkness. His world was a series of sodium-vapor rest stops and fluorescent-lit parking lots, convenience stores and lonely gas pumps in the wolf hours. Delivering cargo of dubious origin ... well, that was just the cost. Isaac thought of it as delivering the night mail.

"Twenty minutes," Half Smith said. "WinCo parking lot, by the dry cleaner entrance. Cargo's already inside, keys in the wheel well."

"Anything special?"

Half Smith chuckled again, his voice thick with phlegm. "Don't shake it, don't drop it. It won't blow up, but it's fragile. Everything else is the same."

Isaac nodded. Anything dangerous, Smith probably would have said. For a guy who'd drop you in the desert short a head if he felt like it, he wasn't a bad boss. Work ethic was pretty much the same as any other job, just a lot less legal. Playing the game got you ahead, doing the job right got you ignored. Smith rewarded his loyalty by paying him well and on time, and not sending guys around to ruin his day.

"Get a move on," Smith said. Two clicks, then silence as the call ended. Isaac put his phone in his jeans pocket, pulled on a thick black hoodie, and headed for the door. *Neither rain nor snow*, Isaac thought, and whistled a few notes as he stepped out.

Isaac knew his ride when he saw it. Usually, he got a mid-range sedan of some kind, now and then a rice burner, but he'd had utility vans before, like the one waiting for him under the flickering white glow of a lamppost. Long and muddy brown, no markings on the side, undistinguished but clean, a fish-eye rear-view mirror bolted to the driver's side door. Perfect. He pulled the keys from their magnetic resting place, and opened the back door to check on the cargo.

Cargo netting was strung across the width of the van, holding a large cardboard box securely in place. The box took nearly all the available space behind the second bench row seats. Whoever packed it wasn't worried about people opening the box, as it had been taped closed enough to keep the flaps down, and nothing more. Isaac flicked the netting with a finger. It strummed tautly against the cardboard.

"You ain't going anywhere," Isaac told the box, and slammed the rear door. He climbed into the driver's seat, spent a minute checking around the dash to figure out where all the controls were. Satisfied, he shut the door and started the van. It purred to life without a hitch, and Isaac backed out into the WinCo lot, shifted into drive and headed onto the road, finding his space in the holes and patterns of evening traffic.

Once past the garish battlements of the mall, and its moat of restaurants and boutiques, other drivers petered out, and Isaac fell into the hypnotic flow of interstate traffic. Heading southeast, he sped up, weaving between ponderous Macks and Peterbilts, feeling the rumbles of their passing as they fell behind him. Walls of light bloomed and faded in his rearview mirror. Isaac smiled. He was on the move.

The night mail doesn't have to stay close to home, he thought. Smith had never offered him any promises on that score. The work was enough. Isaac had little use for money. His life in the daylight hours was nothing more than maintenance: sleeping, eating, minutiae. Whatever Isaac was beyond that was all out on the road. There, Isaac was a prince of motion, cloaked in the perfume of unleaded and hot rubber.

Within moments, Isaac found himself comfortably alone on the freeway. He leaned back in his seat, feeling the familiar glow of comfort flow through him. He flicked on the stereo, the one-touch keys and a clear display making it easy to surf, and the speakers were pretty good for a cargo van. This close to Boise, he could still pick up what few half-decent stations were in town, mostly classic rock. Around the middle of the dial, he found a station that seemed to be stuck in the 70s, and let a raft of cheese rock fill the van as the road wound on. Before long, despite himself, Isaac found himself singing along. In the back of the van, wrapped securely in netting and the cardboard box, Isaac's cargo sat quietly, unmoved by Isaac's approximation of "Locomotive Breath" and the jostling of the freeway.

*   *   *

Despite a name that sounded like trucker porn, the Gearjammer was one of the few truck stops where Isaac felt at ease. Most of the truckers Isaac met were outgoing, loud men, talking to the room as if everyone were friends. At the Gearjammer, though, people tended to keep to themselves. They went to the restaurant for chicken-fried steak and bitter coffee, fueled up at the pumps outside, stopped in the shop long enough to get jerky and Pepsi, and were gone. People passed through the Gearjammer with purpose, and Isaac was on board.

At a little after nine, the place was busy as usual. Isaac strode past the candy aisles and the cooler wall, stepping around a young woman, slim and pierced, who seemed to be weighing the benefits of Doritos vs. Lays. A lanky, acne-riddled teen was running a mop in the back by the restrooms, occasionally sneaking a glance at the pierced girl, whose shirt didn't reach the waist of her low-slung jeans. Isaac noted it all absently; he needed a bathroom break, a hard shot of caffeine, and to get back on the road, in that order.

Isaac opened the men's room door, intent on relieving the ache in his bladder, and stopped. One of Half Smith's enforcers, a bullet-shaped bruiser named Don, was standing by the sink, looking at Isaac as if he were running slightly late. Since Don generally worked the west side of Boise, the fact that he was there at all was a surprise. Don doled out the punishment of a wrathful Half, and Isaac had never done anything to merit harsh language, much less Don.

"Isaac," Don said, as if they regularly met in truck stop restrooms. A Larry Craig joke came to mind, but Isaac's good sense kept him quiet. It wasn't that Don didn't have a sense of humor. Just the opposite: Don had a wickedly unpredictable sense of humor. In fact, Don was known to plan things out in order to share his funny with a victim. Isaac only knew the details of one such joke—using a debtor's own dentures to bite off a finger, after which the guy seemed deliriously happy to cough up money—but he'd heard rumors of others, including what one of Half's minions had darkly referred to as "the wheelchair gag."

"Don," Isaac said, forcing calm into his voice as he stepped to the urinal. "I didn't think you came out this way much."

"There's been a change in the dance card," Don said. "Half decided to move the cargo to a different location, and it needs diplomacy more than driving. I'll take it from here."

"But--" Isaac said, his pride hurt. He didn't mind being passed over for work, but starting a job only to have it taken from him stung. It wasn't like he was out of touch. Half knew Isaac had his phone with him, and cell service was good for at least an hour down the interstate. Why hadn't he called?

Don cut him off. "Half's got better things to do than hold a driver's hand."

"Yeah," Isaac said, moving to the sink, and wondering what the hell he was going to do with the rest of his night. Without the drive, he could sit around his apartment listening to Mexican hip-hop through the floor, or find a bar to be lonely in.

"Let's get the cargo. Half told me to pay you for the night, so I'll give you your money and you can drive home. Park the van at your place. Half will tell you where to drop it off tomorrow," Don said, and motioned Isaac out. Isaac wanted to argue, but what was the point? If Half didn't want him to finish the job, he wasn't going to finish. Isaac dried his hands and fell in step with Don.

A hot breeze, smelling of diesel and sage, greeted them as they reached the parking lot. Besides the pierced girl, slouched against the front wall by the newspaper machines, there was nobody around. Isaac could see the pimply mop manager through the plate window, the flickering light from a small TV painting his face in shadow.

Don reached the cargo door of the van first. He reached for the handle, but stopped short. A funny expression, part smile, and part facial shrug, rippled across Don's broad face. He half-turned to Isaac and theatrically bowed, gesturing to the door. "After you."

Isaac shrugged and opened the door, wondering what had Don in such a strange mood. Maybe Don was getting a fat bonus for taking the box to wherever the hell he was going. The netting was still taut across the box's front. Isaac reached for the clasp that held the top in place.

From the driver's side came a girl's voice, husky but feminine. "Hey! What the fuck?!?"

Isaac glanced up to see the pierced girl standing by the van, eyes hooded, but her face in a familiar, "I can't believe I'm seeing this shit," expression. She held something in her right hand, tensed as if to swing. Above his head, shadows shifted. Intuition spun Isaac around.

Don was standing behind Isaac, his right arm high over his head, a heavy lead teardrop in his hand. The girl's shout made him hesitate. Isaac recoiled and fell into the cargo box.

"Fuck," Isaac said, holding his hands out. His ass started to slip off its perch, and he drew his leg up, pulling it inside the van. Isaac was almost on his side against the box, and Don still hadn't decided which way to swing.

"Hell with it," Don said, and reached forward to grab Isaac's shirt. Muscles like sandbags rippled in his arm. Isaac tried to leap to his feet, but fell backward. With adrenaline and panic, he kicked against the open cargo door. The door shot forward, stopping with a crunch when it collided with Don's face.

Isaac had never seen anyone take a serious hit in the face, but he was sure Don's nose was broken, and his cheekbone had an oddly sunken look. As Don sprawled on the asphalt, Isaac heard a light clicking that sounded exactly like broken teeth hitting the ground. The smell of wet copper hung in a cloud.

"Oh shit," the girl said. "That must have hurt."

Isaac turned to face her. She'd looked pretty enough in the store, but under the harsh orange lamps of the parking lot, her face seemed older, more haggard. Her eyes sparkled feverishly in the shadows. Was she excited? She had warned him, so he owed her for that.

"Thanks," Isaac said, making sure Don wasn't getting up. Turning your back on him was a bad, bad idea. *Wheelchair gag,* Isaac thought. "For the warning."

"You gonna call the cops?" the girl asked, looking over at the c-store. Nobody had come outside since Isaac and Don, but that wouldn't last. Even if the Gearjammer didn't have cameras out front, the parking lot wasn't secluded. Someone would notice a guy with a busted nose and broken teeth lying unconscious on the asphalt, and then Isaac would have a whole new set of problems.

"Not for this," Isaac said. "He's just one of my pissy co-workers."

"Come on, man. This dude's obviously an enforcer, and you're a driver. Unless you're driving this guy to work, I ain't seeing your paths crossing much."

"What the hell would you know?"

The girl shrugged. "I been in the life. What can I say?"

Isaac looked down at Don, who hadn't moved since he fell. Under the fluorescent lights outside the entrance, he pulled out his cell. He speed-dialed Half, and waited for enlightenment.

"Yes?" The voice was rough, used to giving orders. It wasn't Half Smith.

Isaac froze. The sound of freeway traffic, trucks and lonely cars rolling toward destinations unknown, washed over Isaac and across cellular airwaves.

"You still have the cargo, Mr. Ericsson." The voice was flat now, harder.

"Uh," Isaac said, "where's Half?"

Silence. Isaac counted heartbeats, reached eight before the voice spoke. "Indisposed." Menace seeped from every unyielding syllable.

"Where is Don?" the voice asked.

Isaac looked down at his feet. Don was still, a thin worm of blood etching its way down his cheek, forming a growing pool on the asphalt. "He's taking a breather. Long day."

"Put him on," the voice commanded.

"I'll have him call you back in a minute," Isaac said, and disconnected. "Shit."

"Your boss is pissed," the girl said.

"My boss is dead," Isaac said, thinking about what that meant. Did Half have anything about him written down? Was there a file in a box somewhere that gave the breadth and width of his life to whoever killed Half? Isaac imagined a pair of enforcers, big and bullet-shaped like Don, sitting in the shadows around his apartment, listening to his neighbors' music and waiting for Isaac to appear. He shuddered.

"Well, then," the girl said after a minute, "you'll need a new job."

*   *   *

In a generic earth-tone office in a generic strip mall somewhere on the northwest side of Boise, a gloved hand put a sleek black handset back into its cradle, cutting off the sound of empty circuits. The owner of the gloved hand and the rough voice sat behind a desk that had, until earlier that evening, belonged to a mid-league crime manager known as Half Smith. On the floor directly in front of the desk, a large blue tarp was spread out to cover an area roughly twice the desk's size. Over that, another equally large stretch of plastic sheeting was laid, and on top of that, lay a battered Half Smith, nude and bleeding to death from the jagged stumps of his fingers and a scattering of slashes along his torso and legs. Half was a man of strong character and deep reserves of will, but his reluctance to speak had ended with the loss of his left ring finger. Unfortunately, the gloved man had not ordered Half's de-fingering to get him to talk. He just didn't want fingerprints to identify the body.

"Now, boss?" one of the gloved man's enforcers asked, a pillar of muscle gifted with the power of speech. He held a black-handled pair of pliers in one hand, fingers like tree roots dwarfing the tool in his grip. *How can he even use those,* the gloved man wondered.

A strangled sound came from the plastic. It came again, and the gloved man realized that Smith was trying to laugh. "You'll be here a while," Smith wheezed through torn and bloodied lips. "I've got all my teeth. Never had a cavity."

The gloved man raised an eyebrow. That was good to know. Healthy teeth would come out, of course, but it could take a while. The night was wearing on, and they still had to pick up Smith's last cargo shipment from the simpleton he'd been using for years to make deliveries.

"Get the bat," the gloved man told the other bodyguard, just as imposing and impassive as his colleague. "Loosen his teeth before using the pliers."

A choked laugh came up from the floor. Half Smith was tougher than they'd thought; most of those who'd received a beating like Half's tended to die in the middle, and nobody who lived as long as Half was in a laughing mood. The second bodyguard decided his first swing would put out Half's lights for good.

"Mr. Smith, you seem extraordinarily amused," the gloved man said.

"I know something you don't know, fucker," Half said through swollen lips. "You're going to be surprised."

"Oh? Save us both the suspense and tell me what it is."

"Not much profit for me," Half said. "Got something to offer?"

The gloved man shrugged lightly. "We'll see if you have a quid for my quo."

With that, the gloved man leaned down. Both bodyguards were in motion before his Saville Row suit touched the carpet, but he held up one hand. Carefully, the gloved man loomed over Half's abused body until their heads were nearly touching. Half Smith cleared his throat, lifted his head a few inches above the plastic sheeting, and whispered his last words to the gloved man, a low susurration the bodyguards heard like a soft trickling of water. Then the whispering stopped, and Smith let his head drop with a soft thud.

"Boss?" the first bodyguard said.

The gloved man stood slowly, smoothing the wrinkles in the navy-blue fabric. He seemed unconcerned with whatever revelation Smith had made. A handful of seconds passed before the gloved man adjusted his suit to his satisfaction and moved to the corner of the office. A matte-black composite Rawlings baseball bat rested against the wall. The gloved man picked up the bat, swung it deftly a few times.

"Nice weight," he said.

He walked back to the plastic sheeting, bat in hand, and looked down at Smith. Every pass of the bat made a whirring sound, a hum of expectant power and force, promising home runs and long triples against the back field wall. Neither bodyguard had seen a bat used for a baseball game in years.

The gloved man raised the bat over his head, samurai-style.

"Quid pro quo," the gloved man said, and brought the bat down with a muscular swing.

*   *   *

The girl was still standing by the van when Isaac came back from dumping Don in an unused corner of the lot. She'd lit a cigarette, the dirty orange ember glowing in the knife-edged shadows around the van. "He still alive?"

"Yep," Isaac said. "Good thing. I don't need any more trouble than I got."

"Sure," the girl said. Smoke billowed around her, rose and danced in the sharp fluorescent light.

"Thanks for your help," Isaac said.

"Can I get a lift?" the girl asked. With a flick of her wrist, she spun the cigarette butt far out into the wide lot. Traffic noise was no more than an occasional rush of tires and engines, and the quiet surrounding them put Isaac's nerves more on edge.

"Where you headed?" the girl asked.

"Tremonton," Isaac finally said. He'd expected the girl to ask where the hell that was, but she nodded, or appeared to in the gloom. She stepped into the light, her apparent age dropping back to barely legal, maybe ten years younger than Isaac.

"Mace," she said, offering Isaac her hand.

"Isaac," he said. He shook her hand curtly. It was warm and hard, a heated rock wrapped in skin. He tried not to look surprised. "Climb in."

Over the western horizon, Isaac could see a massing of thunderclouds. A little storm action made no difference to him—he loved driving in the rain—but enough thunder and lightning would screw up radio reception this far out. He figured he had maybe until the next canyon, about five miles east, until he lost the Boise stations.

Miles ticked by, tires humming in counterpoint to the steady wind outside. It was a soothing sound, one that lulled Mace into a fitful doze that deepened as the van continued eastward. Isaac felt himself slip into the zone. A few drops spattered against the windshield, random at first, then falling faster like divine bullets. Ten minutes outside the Hagerman exit, bullets turned to sheets, scattering visibility and turning the van into a drum. The rattle shook Mace awake, and she sat up straight.

"Wow," Mace said as they passed the on-ramp. "Hasn't rained like this in a long time."

"Storm's coming up behind us," Isaac said. He turned the wheel a fraction of a heartbeat before the van's tires slid on the water gathering in I-84's ruts, stopping the fishtail before it could become more than a splash. Rain pooled on the road, joining potholes and frost heaves into a scattered sea.

"Is it going to be like this all the way to Tremonton?" Mace asked.

Isaac flicked her a look, but the road was too wet and rough to look away for long. "You're not planning on staying there, are you?"

Mace shrugged. "Nowhere better to go. Maybe I'll go on to Salt Lake, maybe hitch over to Denver."

"Wrong time of year to hitch through the mountains," Isaac said. A stray bolt of wind shook the van, changing the pattern of the fantails and spray across the windows and windshield. Storms didn't frighten Isaac, but this one might be more than he wanted to drive in.

"No right time," Mace said, staring into the storm's teeth as Isaac drove.

Around and over them, the stars disappeared behind a great floor of clouds and rain, coating the sky as thick as silence.

A nova-white crack of lightning flared, searing the night and causing Isaac to go briefly, terrifyingly blind. Retinal after-images sparked as he blinked furiously, trying to focus on the world before his headlights. There was little traffic on the road, and the stretch of freeway they were on was straight, but this was Idaho, after all. Animals of all sizes and shapes wandered onto freeways here.

From the seat next to him, Isaac heard whispering. He turned to ask his passenger to speak up, and understood she was counting to herself, just like he had been taught. Counting the seconds between the flash and the rumble to see how far away the strike had been.

" ... two-Mississippi, three-Mississ—"

Like the hand of an angry God, the thunder broke on the roof of the van. Its passage made the van ring, a hollow flexing sound like a wounded bull's bellow. Pressure roared in Isaac's ears like gunfire in a bell jar. His head was exploding, but he kept the van straight.

Another lightning tree tore the darkness, and Isaac's world went white. He blinked furiously, the sudden darkness edged with purple streaks, and realized he was completely blind. Beside him, he heard Mace breathe in sharply; their van was drifting, and they stood a good chance of flipping if he went off the road.

For the first time ever, Isaac was completely disoriented behind the wheel. The vibrations of the road told him he was still moving, but they could be about to hit a mountain for all he knew.

A warm hand closed over his, pushing the steering wheel left a few degrees. He started to pull away, but Mace closed her fingers over his tightly, keeping the wheel steady. Subtly, a change in vibration told him the wheels had slipped into ruts on the freeway, and he realized she could see the road. Isaac's vision was still a whirlwind of purple and ghost shapes, and he let himself be led, knowing that otherwise, he'd probably crash and kill them both. He applied brakes gently, letting the speed run down as Mace guided them. She tapped his hand, and he carefully brought the van to a stop, fumbling into park and turning the engine off.

Isaac sat back, his now-damp shirt giving him a sudden chill. His vision was slowly returning; he could make out the faint glow of the dashboard, the spray of headlights through sheets of water tumbling down the windshield. Mace was still leaning over, her hand clutching the wheel, staring out the windshield. He kept his eyes shut for a moment longer than he needed, his forehead against the cool plastic of the steering wheel, before turning the ignition key. The ticking of the engine disappeared, replaced by the rumble of pistons. He stared out at the road. The phantoms and streaks in his vision were gone, at least.

"Okay," he said, and put the van into gear.

"You sure you up to driving, Stevie Wonder?" Mace said. She looked tiny, huddled in the seat beneath a thin denim jacket she'd pulled from the frayed knapsack by her feet. Hard to believe this was the same girl who'd been ready to sock an enforcer.

Isaac smiled, and pulled out onto the freeway. Traffic was still almost nothing, a pair of lonely semis in the westbound lanes their only companions for the moment. "I'll roll down the window and drive by sound, if it makes you feel better."

Mace nodded and turned her gaze outward through the passenger window and over the indistinct desert. The land they drove through was mostly scrub and hills, dotted with fences, and lonely lights on poles guarding ranch houses and workshops, a landscape indifferent to its settlers and ignorant of its passerby.

"What's the story with your box back there?" Mace said. Isaac didn't take his eyes off the road. After the westbound trucks vanished over a hill, there were no other vehicles on the freeway. Except for the steady pulse of lights from a plane overhead, they were the only things moving for miles. The stillness was oppressive. His gaze flicked over at her.

"I don't know what's in it," he finally said. "My boss didn't say."

"Didn't you say your boss was dead?" Mace asked.

"He is now," Isaac said. "He wasn't when I picked it up earlier. He is…well, he was pretty good about telling me what I needed to know about cargo without telling me what I didn't."

"Seems he left something out about this run," Mace said.

"Asking too many questions of a guy like Half Smith isn't a good idea."

"Half Smith? I know that guy," Mace said, sitting up in her seat. "He used to come into the club where I danced."

"You're a dancer?" Isaac asked.

"Was," Mace said. "Not much future in it, so I quit. Why? You surprised a girl like me could get a job getting naked for money?"

"Every dancer I ever met looked beef jerky off the stage," Isaac said, his mouth racing ahead without help from his brain. "Used up, dried up, and bitter. You don't seem like any of that. Well, maybe bitter."

Mace laughed. "I'm not bitter. Just cynical. There's a difference."

"It's a fancier word," Isaac agreed. "I'll give you that."

"Thanks," Mace said, still smiling. "A girl has to maintain her illusions."

Isaac nodded, but said nothing. An off-ramp swam out of the rain, now slowed to barely more than a drizzle. He signaled out of habit and took the exit. About a mile or so from the ramp, a single convenience store blazed with the power of a few run-down fluorescent lamps, still outshining the ranch lights speckled here and there. Mace stretched and sighed.

"You get paid a lot for this?" she asked.

"I ain't rich, but I do all right," Isaac said. "I'm hoping that by doing this job quick and right, the new boss doesn't feel like giving me the Smith treatment."

"Meaning dead," Mace said.

"That's the hope," Isaac said. "I talked to the guy after we knocked out Don. Not the best odds. What else can I do?"

"Not to be a jerk, but *we* didn't knock out that guy. You and the cargo door did that," Mace said.

"That's what I meant," Isaac said. The c-store was open, but the lot was empty. Except for a shadow behind the counter, there was nobody around. Isaac, who'd been driving throughout the state for years, was used to the population going to ground after nightfall. If he saw more than three cars at a c-store after 11, the place was getting robbed.

He pulled into the closest non-handicapped parking space to the door, turned off the van, and climbed out. Together, Isaac and Mace went inside.

*   *   *

"Sir, I don't know how we're going to catch them," Rutherford said, his professional gaze finding nothing in the scrub brush outside his window. They were several exits past the Gearjammer, and going faster than seemed smart. Wheeler swapped lanes as they approached curves, avoiding frost heaves with surgical swerves. Rutherford knew his partner was an excellent driver, but any trooper scanning the roads would be sure to see the Infiniti in dollar signs.

"One of the nuggets Smith passed on before he passed on," the gloved man said, "was that his driver was a man of structure and habit. He'll stop every hour or so unless he's on a timetable, and he'll follow a general routine. He'll stay with his routine in the belief that by following his assigned task, he will curry favor with the new administration."

"He does have a head start on us, sir," Wheeler pointed out. "Even given his general behavior, we could be too far behind to catch up before he reaches Tremonton."

"Possibly," the gloved man said, "but I don't think we'll have too much trouble finding him. Not all exits have facilities, and I imagine he thinks I'm in Boise, awaiting his return."

Rutherford looked at his partner, who shrugged nonchalantly and returned his eyes to the road. "Did you bring anything besides your nine?" Wheeler asked Rutherford quietly.

Rutherford nodded. "Pen blade and piano wire. You?"

Wheeler shrugged. "Just the stiletto. Haven't used it in a while."

Rutherford snorted. "You do love the classics."

"Hey, it's got reach," Wheeler said. "Besides, piano wire? This ain't Luca Brasi we're going after."

"It's useful stuff," Rutherford said.

"Oh, yeah," Wheeler sneered, "it's the Swiss army knife of assassins."

"A, we're not assassins," Rutherford said, "we're enforcers. Assassins kill people as their only job. It's just an extra service we offer. B, the Swiss army knife is the Swiss army knife of assassins. You can kill somebody with damn near anything in one of those jobbies."

"Toothpick?" Wheeler said.

"You can't kill somebody with a toothpick?" Rutherford said. Wheeler's face didn't change, but his knuckles were turning white on the steering wheel.

"Can you?" Wheeler snapped.

"Never tried," Rutherford said. "I did jam one in a guy's tear duct once, turned him into Chatty Cathy."

"So, you don't know if you can kill somebody with a toothpick," Wheeler said.

"Nope, but I don't rule it out either," Rutherford said. "I remain open to the possibility."

"That's very New Age of you," Wheeler said. "Me, I want to get the job done."

"And pull some teeth," Rutherford pointed out.

"There is that," Wheeler allowed.

"You're a sick bastard, Wheeler." Wheeler nodded and grinned. They worked well together.

"Take the next exit," the gloved man said, startling his enforcers.

"Sir?" Wheeler said as he signaled.

The gloved man pointed over Rutherford's broad shoulder. "Parked in front of that convenience store. Mr. Ericsson did indeed keep to his patterns."

Wheeler pulled the Infiniti smoothly up to the parking space farthest from the van, and stopped. Both men paused, their hands on the door handles.

"Orders, sir?" Rutherford asked, his eyes on the c-store entrance. Wheeler's gaze was locked on the van. His stare was unblinking, intense.

"Check the van first," the gloved man said. "Wheeler, you go inside and see if you can find Mr. Ericsson. Bring him outside and take care of him. Rutherford, you stay close by. We'll make sure the cargo is undamaged before we take it out."

"Yes, sir," the enforcers replied in unison, and stepped out into the night, the gloved man at their heels. Had anyone in the store looked outside at that moment, they would have seen a pair of shadows in suits, weapons in their hands as they moved closer to the light, preceding a darker shadow that revealed nothing.

*   *   *

All convenience stores are lit like prison cells, Isaac thought, as he and Mace wandered the store's squat aisles. Why convenience stores chose to use the same lighting scheme, Isaac didn't know.

It was a serious downside to his job, spending so much time in stores lit by these damn piercing lamps.

"Caffeine?" Mace said, waving her hand at the cooler wall along the back of the store.

"Please," Isaac said. He pointed at a large beige machine with a faded picture of a large coffee cup on the front, red handles in a row below the picture. "I think hot is the way to go tonight. Want some? I'm buying."

"Thanks, Richie Rich, but I'm sticking with Mountain Dew," Mace said. She grabbed a bag of something crunchy off the shelf to her right, held it up. "They have these available in sour cream and onion, or nacho cheese. What would be your pleasure, m'sieu?"

An electronic tone sounded, the standard for convenience stores everywhere Isaac had ever been. He turned and looked out of habit, expecting to see the clerk—a thin Mexican woman with a tattoo on her arm—walking back in from her smoke break, and instead, a tall, bullet-shaped man with close-cropped hair and the unmistakable carriage of muscle stepped inside. Everything about the man—the way he walked, the dark suit, the grim blankness of his face—screamed enforcer. The man's eyes scanned the store rapidly, pausing on Mace's back for a fraction of a moment, and coming to rest on Isaac, who was standing by the coffee machines two aisles away from the registers and the front door.

The enforcer smiled. His teeth were shockingly white, even, perfect. *Those can't be real,* a part of Isaac's mind piped up. *They're almost art.*

"Mr. Ericsson," the enforcer said in a clear, bemused tone. "We've been looking for you."

"We?" Isaac said, his heart hammering in his chest. First Don, now this guy.

"My partner and I, per our boss's request," said the enforcer. "In fact, he's here now. He'd like to speak to you. Outside."

Fuck, Isaac thought. Stepping outside would be the end of him. They might not pop him here, but they probably drove here in something with a trunk. If there was anybody here, the smart thing to do would have been make some noise, see if he could bring the law, but the clerk was gone and Mace—

Isaac made a show of yawning and took a quick look around as he stretched. She'd disappeared from view. Smart girl. Maybe she'd keep off their radar, and they'd never know she was there. No point in getting her involved, probably killed, just because she'd needed a lift. Isaac decided to play it professional, hoping killing him made less sense from a business perspective than keeping him on, or just letting him loose.

"Okay," he said. "Let's speak to the boss." He walked past the enforcer, expecting a rough hand to grab him and pull him along. Instead, the bullet-shaped man stepped aside and allowed Isaac to go through the door first. Once through the door, Isaac saw why; a second enforcer was waiting, similarly muscled and a little taller, in front of a third man, lean and well-attired, standing aloof by the van, whose back door stood open.

"Evening," Isaac said as he approached carefully, hands open and at his sides. No frisking or beating ensued. Instead, the second enforcer stepped aside, taking up position at Isaac's elbow. The third man stood before Isaac, examining him in the harsh store lights. Isaac had the sensation of being X-rayed, scanned to a molecular level by something huge and glacial. It was unpleasant, and Isaac realized who the man was.

"Mr. Ericsson," the gloved man said, flexing his fingers.

Isaac's mind blanked. Smith had been unnerving at times, but the gloved man was different. He had a predatory quality, like the distillation of every eating machine on the savannah.

"Your services will no longer be required," the gloved man told Isaac, motioning to the open van and the closed trunk of the car parked next to it.

"You can always find use for a good driver," Isaac said calmly. Any hope he had was in keeping a professional demeanor. "Nobody knows what I carry except whoever needs to know. Me, I don't need to know. I don't even know what I was carrying tonight."

The gloved man stared at Isaac. "A pity. One's curiosity should be settled before losing the chance to satisfy it."

From his left, the whisper of steel from a hidden sheath. An answering sound, like threads of a screw scraping past each other, echoed on his right. His right elbow was caught in a monstrous grip. No escape that way, Isaac knew, not with the enforcer squeezing pain into his nerves. He worked up his courage, planning to slam his left elbow into the other guy with all the power he could manage.

The electronic tone of the door sounded again. Isaac turned his head to see, and felt his heart sink as Mace walked into view.

The enforcer looked down at her. His face twisted into an expression that might have been surprise, disgust, or an overwhelming urge to sneeze. "Mace?"

"Hey Wheeler," she said. "See you and Ruthie are still with Beelzebub there." She flicked a hand at the gloved man. "What's up with that? Don't you have any entrepreneurial spirit?"

"Not your concern, Mace," Ruthie said. "We're on business here, nothing to get involved in."

"It really isn't," Mace said. "Still, here I am."

"I remember you," the gloved man said. His eyes, cold as a black dwarf star, never left Mace. "You were quite the stripper, as I recall."

"Interpretive dancer," Mace said. "Performance artist. Burlesque professional, if you must. Stripper is so mundane. You remove paint with it."

"A rose by any other name," the gloved man said.

"You've got your cargo," Mace said. "Why don't you let Isaac be on his way?"

For a moment, the gloved man appeared to consider the idea. His gaze, serene and elegant without warmth, turned inward, long enough for Isaac to wonder what kind of razor-blade landscapes the gloved man saw inside himself.

The gloved man looked at Isaac. His eyes held nothing. Isaac tensed his biceps, preparing to throw all he had into one desperate elbow into Ruthie's gut. From the look of the guy, Isaac thought he might die with a chipped elbow, but his options were limited.

Mace sighed. "Damn it," she said, looking up as if to find guidance in the stars. Now she turned and faced the gloved man. "Why do you always do this?" she asked him.

Surprisingly, the gloved man shrugged. "This is how the world works. Loose ends. I could write you an equation to explain why he is a risk."

"He knows nothing," Mace said.

"But now he knows that he knows nothing," the gloved man said. "I wonder why you care?"

"Contempt," Mace said, and without any sign, pivoted on one foot and spun around in a slashing move. A solid kick slammed into the inside of Wheeler's knee. The snapping sound was immediate, sickening. Isaac actually felt the vibration of cartilage and tendon breaking under the blow. Wheeler's leg gave way, and with a curse, he started to fall, letting go of Isaac's arm in surprise. Isaac staggered under the sudden release of pressure and stumbled into Ruthie, already in motion. Isaac managed to tangle himself in the enforcer's legs, bringing them both to the pavement with a hard thump.

Wheeler was down on the ground, his battered leg now at an angle that hurt the eye. He jackknifed to a sitting position, and with surprising speed, swung the stiletto in a short arc at Mace's legs. Her foot came up faster, stopping Wheeler's swing short. Another snap, Wheeler's wrist now. The stiletto flew from his grip, sparkling dully as it spun, clattering to a rest near the front of the store. Mace's foot rebounded and launched into a powerful front kick that ended in Wheeler's skull. A deep, wet crunch sounded as the boot drove cartilage into his brain. Slowly he fell backward, striking his head on the pavement.

Isaac lurched to a near-standing position, raised his good arm, and half-falling, struck Ruthie in the right kidney as hard as he could. The enforcer cried out, and sprawled on his stomach, his face bouncing off the asphalt. Isaac pushed off with his good arm, and took an elbow to the chin before he could strike again. His teeth clacked together and a grinding jolt slammed into his skull, but he didn't lose consciousness. He pounded the enforcer on the back savagely, a wild symphony of fist and elbow, until he landed a thump to the back of Ruthie's head, knocking the enforcer unconscious.

Isaac fell on Ruthie's stunned body, pain and adrenaline fighting it out in his veins. He raised his gaze to see Mace and the gloved man facing each other like gunfighters. Mace looked sweaty and pissed, and Isaac wondered what kind of dancing you had to do to be able to kick people like that.

"That was … poorly chosen," the gloved man said finally.

"Consider that a favor," Mace said. "Ruthie's still alive. You're only short one sick fuck."

"He was a useful sick fuck," the gloved man said. "Do you think you can kick me to death, too?"

Mace glared at the gloved man. "Well, you might have to get your hands dirty," Mace said, "gloves or no gloves."

The gloved man shrugged, but before the gesture was completed, he flew into motion. Isaac's jaw dropped; the gloved man was *fast*. Something in his hand was inches from Mace's face before Isaac could blink. She ducked, moved inside the gloved man's reach, jabbed stiffened fingers at his throat. He dodged, but not quite enough. The graze of her fingers drew blood, and Isaac heard the strike in his breathing.

Suddenly, Mace was spun to the side, a red fist mark clear on her face. She stumbled backward as the gloved man pressed forward, his hands empty now, but moving in short, brutal arcs. Mace dodged the second punch, threw one that caught the point of his chin and rocked him back a few paces. He fetched up hard against the van. The impact knocked the breath from him, but he lunged forward and struck her hard below the ribs. The punch lifted Mace off her feet and pushed her back, but she didn't fall.

"You're a tough one," the gloved man said. "I may keep you around after all this."

"I worked for you once already," Mace said. "You're a terrible boss."

Isaac looked around for a weapon. She was tough, but the gloved man was something else. Mace could kick an enforcer's ass, and she was having a hard time with this guy. Isaac knew the gloved man would make short work of him, so he needed an edge. In Ruthie's jacket, he found one.

The gloved man took a boxing stance, threw a pair of jabs at Mace. She blocked one, ducked the second, and went for his eyes. The gloved man doubled over as her real intent—a knee strike—caught him in the solar plexus, driving all the air from his lungs. He fell to his knees.

"You should die," Mace said to the gloved man. He opened his mouth to speak and vomited instead, a long rush of fluid onto the gritty asphalt. His back arched as he tried to rock back on his knees and face Mace. Isaac stepped behind him with the Glock 9mm he had pulled from Ruthie's holster, and clubbed the gloved man on the back of the head. Unconscious, the gloved man fell forward, scraping his face along the grit and sprawling headlong in his own vomit.

Isaac stared for a long minute, the pistol in his hand. Finally, he looked at Mace, who was staring at Isaac in disbelief.

"What the fuck?" Mace said. "Are you trying to piss him off? When he wakes up with a splitting headache lying in his own puke, he'll move killing your ass to the top of his to-do list."

"I drive," Isaac said, his arm still blazing from Wheeler's monstrous hold. "I move stolen goods. I work with bad people. I get paid in blood money. I do not kill. It's that simple."

"How principled of you," Mace said, her eyes narrowing. "He'll admire that about you when he's skinning your carcass."

Isaac tucked the Glock in his waistband, pulled the back of his shirt out and over his jeans. "Didn't say I wasn't going to hurt him, though."

"Yeah?" Mace said. "I've got a few ideas I'd like to try. Think there's jumper cables in the van?"

Isaac shook his head. "He already moved the cargo into his car, right? Let's go see what His Satanic Majesty wanted so damn bad, and go from there. Which one of these guys you think drove?"

Mace pointed to Wheeler. Isaac fished out the keys, while Mace checked both unconscious men, kicking the gloved man in the ribs to make sure he wasn't faking. They walked to the car and popped the trunk. The box sat there, alone in the spacious cargo bay.

"Let's see what we got," Isaac said. He held the Glock steady over the box, finger on the trigger guard, and slowly reached forward with his other hand to open the box.

"You wouldn't shoot the bastard trying to kill you, but you're ready to open fire on a box?" Mace asked.

"I knew what kind of guy he is," Isaac said. "I have no idea what's in this box."

Mace held her breath as Isaac opened one flap, then pulled back the others in succession, exposing the box's contents to the trunk light. They stared down at what lay inside.

"Is that what I think it is?" Isaac said, finally.

"I ... don't know," Mace said. She turned, and walked away from the trunk toward the gloved man. "Let's ask him."

"Wait--" Isaac said, too late to stop Mace from delivering a vicious kick to the gloved man's side. He groaned but didn't come to.

"Mace, stop," Isaac said, as Mace reared back her leg.

"What the hell for?" Mace said, whirling to face Isaac. "You have any idea what this bastard is capable of doing? We kill him now, no worries. You want to look over your shoulder your whole life?"

Isaac sighed. From a pragmatic standpoint, Mace was right. Killing the gloved man was the smart thing to do.

A thought occurred to Isaac then, a touch of sadism evoked or inspired by the gloved man's presence. He looked over at the gloved man's car, then looked at Mace.

"Whatever that thing in the trunk is, he followed me here to get it, wanted to kill me just because I drove it here. Just because I might have seen it."

"So?"

"Seems like something pretty important. You seem to have a serious mad-on for this guy, right?"

"Yeah, but that ain't--" Mace started to say, then stopped talking. Isaac watched the idea bloom across her face, lighting up her eyes. It lifted the years from her face, made her pretty. Isaac felt a momentary rush of discomfort at how it happened, but he'd take what he could get.

"I like where you're going," Mace said, smiling now. Isaac returned the smile, and pointed behind him at the island in the middle of the parking lot.

"Those are 24-hour pumps," he said.

Mace laughed. "I'll bring the car around."

*   *   *

The first thing to bring the gloved man from the darkness was the sinus-scraping sting of gasoline. It reached up into his brain, jolting him awake. His body jerked, but barely moved. Wiggling, he understood that he was bound, trussed by someone who knew what they were doing. Someone who'd done this before.

"Mace," the gloved man rasped, his face pressed against the grit and texture of asphalt, "I don't have the words to express how much trouble you've made for yourself."

"Really?" Isaac said, his face lowering into the gloved man's field of view. "I'm sure she'll be very pleased to hear that. She really dislikes you. I'm not sure why, and I don't think I want to know. I bet it was nasty."

"Mr. Ericsson, you truly have no idea what you're doing," the gloved man said. "Your death would have been pleasant, relatively speaking. That option's off the table."

"That's a hell of a negotiating technique you've got there," Isaac said. "Say, speaking of negotiations, what did you do to Half Smith?"

"Loyalty?" the gloved man snorted.

"Research," Isaac said.

"Of course," the gloved man said. "Your new career as a hard man. Far be it from me to stifle a promising career. How much detail do you want?"

"As much as you can stand," Isaac said. "Mace is indisposed for a while, so take your time."

If the gloved man took any pleasure in the saga of torture and agony he and his men visited upon the late Half Smith, his telling didn't show it. He could have been explaining a particularly lengthy business meeting. His account of the beatings, slicing, forced extractions, and eventual death by baseball bat, was almost clinical in its relating of even the tiniest details, blood spatters and scents, cries and defiant gestures. Isaac understood, with a newfound cold clarity, he was lacking a quality needed for this world. Or maybe he possessed something the gloved man lacked.

Finally, the gloved man reached the end. Isaac swallowed, nodded once. Though he hadn't liked Smith one way or the other, he'd respected him well enough as a boss. Such a death was … well, even if he deserved it, he didn't deserve that.

"Was it everything you hoped for?" the gloved man said.

"No surprises," Isaac said.

"And now, you'll kill me in revenge," the gloved man sneered.

"We're getting ahead of ourselves," Isaac said, climbing to his feet. "First, I have a little surprise for you."

Mace walked into his field of vision, carrying something in her hand. Across the lot, where the highway wound off into an expanse of empty fields, the Infiniti sat, as if parked for an overnight stay. Enough light made its way to the car for the gloved man to see a liquid sheen on the car's skin. The night seemed to twinkle around it.

A rush of air escaped the gloved man's lungs, but he said nothing. His expression was empty, a blank slide of alien landscapes. A window into the abyss. Isaac felt the hair on his arms lift and shiver.

"I don't know what you wanted to kill me over," Isaac said, "but whatever else happens, you're not getting it."

Several feet short of the Infiniti, Mace stopped, turned around to face the two men. A sudden flash of white told the gloved man she was smiling. The object in her hand twinkled brassily in the light.

A lighter.

"You're going to beg me," the gloved man said, "for the treatment I gave Smith."

Isaac sniffed the air. "Say, is that gasoline?"

Mace flicked the lighter wheel. Sharp and orange, a flame leaped from the wick, standing bright and warm in her hand. Barely turning, she casually tossed the lighter into a puddle by the car. Flames leaped, swallowing the puddle in a ring, then a wall of orange heat. The flames raced toward the Infiniti, gaining height as the fire stretched in a flowing path.

Isaac expected an explosion when the gas tank caught, but the resulting pillar of fire more than made up for it.

"I should have bought marshmallows," Mace said as she stood beside Isaac, enjoying the pyre of the gloved man's car and cargo. From where they stood, the heat was bearable, even pleasant.

"Good thing it rained," Isaac said.

The gloved man said nothing. Isaac and Mace stood, keeping one eye on the gloved man to make sure he didn't slip his bonds and claw out their hearts with his nails, but he sat in unmoving silence, as if the universe was slowly coming to a stop around him. Mace kept casting her eyes to the road, looking for a pair of lonely headlights pointed their way.

The gloved man laughed. "Did you call the police? Do you expect some county sheriff to come here and rescue you?" His laughter grew, rolling into the air like smoke, mingling with the heat and climbing into the sky.

"Do you have any idea how long you were out?" Mace suddenly asked.

Slowly, the gloved man's laughter tapered off, slowing to a stray chuckle now and then. "No."

"It was a while," Mace said. "Enough time to get a drink, go to the bathroom and make a phone call."

"Very well," the gloved man said, after Mace fell silent. "I'll bite. Who did you call?"

"Oh, I made a call to a small town not too far from the Utah border," Mace said. "It was Isaac's suggestion."

"I bet you didn't know Half Smith had a bunch of brothers," Isaac said. "He comes from a big family over there. I've met one or two of them. None of them are criminal types like Half, but there are a couple who've got a streak of potential lawbreaker in them."

"They seemed very nice on the phone," Mace said, "until we told them Half was dead. They were especially unhappy with how he died."

"Fortunately, since I've met a couple of them before, they were inclined to believe me when I blamed you for his violent death. Plus, since I told them you're involved with the drug trade, which killed another brother...well, they're quite interested in meeting you," Isaac told the gloved man.

As if on cue, a pair of headlights popped into view from the interstate on-ramp. The gloved man cocked an eyebrow at the sight, but showed no reaction otherwise. His face might have been carved from luminescent stone. Isaac knew what he was allowing to be done was a monstrous act, but then, the gloved man was a monster himself. Monstrous acts to dispose of monstrous people seemed fair.

"That's probably them," Mace said. "Nobody else seems to be out this way tonight."

Within moments, a large utility van similar to the one Isaac had driven pulled up beside them. The side door opened as the ignition shut off, and two large men who could have been clones of Half jumped out. They didn't appear to be armed, but they moved like men who were. Isaac knew the type, and wondered if maybe Half wasn't the only member of the Smith family who'd gone into his particular business. Isaac didn't know those two, but he recognized the driver.

"Elias," Isaac said, nodding respectfully. Once, in a discussion of persuasion techniques Isaac happened to be in the room for, Half mentioned that his oldest brother Elias possessed a temper, and the fact he had learned to keep it reined in only made it worse when he finally let it go. From the grim set of his face, Elias was sitting on it pretty tightly.

"Isaac," Elias said, returning the nod. He gestured at the bound man on the ground, lying still but attentive, as if he was taking notes. "This the guy?"

Isaac nodded again, not trusting himself to speak. The man exuded menace like steam, filling the air. Elias, though, was trouble of a different kind. Elias was a hard man to read, and that made Isaac nervous.

"Charles, Edward," Elias said, "get him in the van." The twins picked up the gloved man and threw him into the van like a sack of dog food. He thumped loudly against the bare metal floor, but didn't make a sound. Isaac was sure Mace had busted in a couple of his ribs, but they didn't seem to be bothering him if she had.

"Thanks," Elias said, as the twins climbed in and shut the door. He turned his back on Isaac and Mace, and walked back around the van's snub nose. Climbing in, he started the van and drove off quickly. It trailed ghost clouds of pale dust and grit as it crossed the parking lot, turned onto the highway, and drove toward the interstate, brake lights casting a lurid backward stare at Isaac and Mace until it merged onto the freeway and disappeared from sight.

"You've got quite the mean streak," Mace said as the van disappeared.

"Or something," Isaac said, turning to look at the unconscious bodyguard still sprawled on the ground. "You ready to go?"

"Where?" Mace asked. "Not like you have anything to deliver now. You set the damn thing on fire, remember?"

"I need another job," Isaac said. "Old boss got capped, new boss is about to be. I think I'll leave the burning the cargo bit off my resume, but other than that, I ought to be able to get work. I'm good at my job."

"No references," Mace said.

Isaac shrugged. "I'll make do. First things first, though. Time to head home."

Mace looked thoughtful for a moment, then nodded agreement. "Might as well. There's nothing in Tremonton this time of year anyway, I bet."

They walked back to the van, taking a wide path around the unconscious Ruthie. Within a minute, they were out of the lot, driving west, heading home.

ACKNOWLEDGMENT

Creating a book is a lopsided endeavor for a writer. The writing is often solitary, depending on the writer's tolerance for beta reading as you go and coffee shop noise, but turning that writing into an actual book takes concerted effort from many. Maybe not quite a nation of millions to make a book real, but once you start counting it up, it might not feel far off. Such is the case with the book you're holding or looking at on a screen; if I listed everyone who had a hand in this collection, this section would be the thickest part. Still, there are the usual suspects to round up and mention.

Charlie, Lindsay, and the gang at Montag Press have allowed me to once more send my darlings into the world under the MP banner, and my work is all the better for their unceasing care and dedication. Their work, especially Lindsay's eagle eye and thoughtful suggestions, have rescued me from many embarrassing gaffes and issues; any that are still here are on me. Among the editorial set, longtime friend Jessica Augusstson of Jayhenge Publishing and Bruce Bethke at Stupefying Stories have been sources of support and friendly editorial guidance for many years, and their publications have provided welcome homes to several of the stories herein.

Finally, I'm permanently indebted to my wife Paige, who despite otherwise being sensible and intelligent has put up with me for several decades, and has made my being a working (well... sometimes) writer much less aggravating than it could have been.

ABOUT THE AUTHOR

Brandon Nolta is a writer, editor, and professional curmudgeon living in the boonies of north Idaho, which is really saying something. After earning a couple of college degrees, he went slightly mad. That didn't go anywhere, so he gave it up and started working for respectable companies again, which he still does to pay for his hobbies of eating regularly and having the lights on. His fiction and poetry have appeared in *Stupefying Stories, The Centropic Oracle, New Myths, Amazing Stories,* and a cacophony of other publications. *No Refuge* is his third book with Montag Press, following the 2015 novel *Iron and Smoke* and the 2020 collection *These Shadowed Stars.* He is both a member of Codex and a full member of the SFWA, and belongs to a few other organizations as well, but you probably wouldn't have heard of them.

www.ingramcontent.com/pod-product-compliance
Lightning Source LLC
Chambersburg PA
CBHW032014240626
47153CB00003B/1244